THE HUMAN FACTOR

Adapted from the film

THE HUMAN FACTOR
by Peter Powell and Thomas Hunter

Simon Quinn

The Human Factor

Futura Publications Limited
A Futura Book

A Futura Book

First published in Great Britain in 1975
by Futura Publications Limited

Copyright © 1975 by Martin Smith

ISBN 0 8600 7311 4

Printed in Great Britain by
Hazell Watson & Viney Ltd,
Aylesbury, Bucks

Futura Publications Limited
Warner Road, London SE5

I

Two slices of Wonder Bread dropped into the Proctor-Silex toaster. On the other side of the kitchen, Ann Kinsdale cracked two eggs into a pan. Maxwell House coffee bubbled in a G.E. percolator.

"Mark, Jeffrey . . . Linda! Breakfast!" Ann called.

"Let them take their time," John Kinsdale entered the kitchen. He kissed Ann on the cheek. His hand rested on her waist and turned her for a kiss on the lips. She resisted just a little, smiling.

"I don't want to bend your slide rule."

"You can bend my slide rule anytime."

The eggs in the pan began spitting and she pushed him away.

"Later, tiger, and that's a promise."

She noted with satisfaction that, characteristically, he did check the slide rule and soft lead pencils in his shirt pocket before sitting at the formica-topped dinette, where he automatically arranged the butter and jelly for the most efficient preparation of toast. Not officiously. Efficiently, the way he did everything. Except love, which he did passionately.

John Kinsdale was in his middle forties, but he looked younger. Swimming and tennis kept his stomach flat, he was tanned and the lines on his face were around the corners of his eyes and his smile. He wore his prematurely white hair an inch longer than military length, his eyes were deep blue and untroubled.

Ann was ten years younger, dark-haired and lithe. At seven in the morning, most mothers might have been in housecoats. Ann never was. In a Liberty print blouse, khaki skirt and sandals, she was trim, energetic and surprisingly sexy.

"We're here," Jeffrey ran into the kitchen.

"Because we're here," Mark followed at a dignified walk.

Mark was a fourteen-year-old with the loose, athletic frame of his father. Jeffrey was more like Ann, wiry and dark, one day short of his eleventh birthday. Linda, six, blonde pigtails to her shoulders, entered carrying a floppy cloth doll almost as big as herself. She wandered over to Ann while Mark caught the toast as it popped up. Jeffrey sorted the Frosted Flakes from a variety pack of cereals.

"Big game today?" Kinsdale asked.

"It's been canceled," Mark spread Parkay.

Linda jumped on a stool and her doll's arm waved, knocking a glass off the sink and onto the floor.

"Linda, I told you to leave Shaggydo behind," Ann picked up the glass.

"But it's not broken," Linda pointed to the glass.

"You mustn't take toys to school."

"It's not a toy, it's Shaggydo."

"Why's that?" Kinsdale pursued his conversation with Mark.

"The team from Camp Darby can't get here. There's another strike. Everyone has hiccups, or something."

"John," Ann pleaded, "speak to Linda about taking toys to school."

"Shaggydo," Kinsdale looked severely across the kitchen, "you can't take Linda to school."

Linda broke down in giggles.

After breakfast, Kinsdale returned to his den for his attache case. The house was new, part of a development, and the sound of the kids carried through the relatively thin walls. He didn't mind. Let other fathers read newspapers at the table; more frightening news passed through his attache case than ever hit public print. He slipped on a plaid sport jacket and clamped a laminated plastic ID onto the jacket pocket. In the middle of the ID was a face-front color picture of Kinsdale and around the edges were boxes signifying security areas the bearer was authorized to enter; in Kinsdale's case, every box was checked.

Ann followed him out to the garage.

"Don't forget," she was counting off her fingers, "the Martins . . . ask Bill about insurance, Wednesday."

Kinsdale got behind the wheel of his Alfa Romeo. The Country Squire station wagon was for Ann's chauffeuring duties.

"Eight o'clock sharp for drinks," he grinned.

"Seven-thirty! Come on, be serious. And Jeff's present. Now you have got it?"

"In the office. Don't worry."

"I hope it isn't something complicated. It's his birthday, not yours."

She leaned into the open sports car and kissed him. Kinsdale backed down the driveway into the street.

"Drive carefully," she added, not because he wasn't a much better than average driver but because the warn-

ing was a formula she believed in. Kinsdale blew her a
kiss as he shifted from reverse into first.

Across the street was a delivery van with its hood up.
The driver, apparently working on a stalled motor,
raised his head to look.

The development was a middle-class mix of ranch
houses, quarter-acre lawns, station wagons, swings and
tricycles. Kinsdale coasted at a cautious twenty m.p.h.
until he reached the red-tiled gate of the housing compound, shifted into third gear and let the Alfa Romeo
purr into the highway traffic at sixty.

Today, he was going to ready the destruction of ten
to one hundred thousand lives.

Today, the seconds were ticking away on the rest of
John Kinsdale's life.

II

Once he was on Autoroute 4, Kinsdale could see Vesuvius looming darkly against the bright blue sky. Still active, the volcano would some days loose dark plumes like warning signals. Today, it was still as a ghost. Fiats, Lancias, and Kinsdale's Alfa Romeo curled around the low foothills of the volcano toward what was often called the most beautiful bay in the world.

Autoroute 4 straightened and plunged into Naples, which was itself a jumble of mad color and life pouring into the Mediterranean. On the other side of Vesuvius was Pompeii, once the most animated city of the Roman Empire. With Pompeii dead, the village called Napoli flourished with Pompeii's refugees, who had fled no farther from Vesuvius than their old homes had been. John Kinsdale, twentieth-century American, once ruled out California because of earthquakes. But in the grip of a torrent Neapolitans called life he, too, had accepted a home in the shadow of a living crater.

Sidewalk cafés, clotheslines, palaces, cathedrals,

everything was lightly poised between that ancient
threat of volcanos and the enormous sweep of a glassy
green sea. Kinsdale downshifted and passed one bus
of soldiers and a second bus of nuns. The city rose to
overwhelm the highway. Kinsdale maneuvered by the
Central Railroad station and circled the Piazza
Garibaldi to the boulevard of the Corso Umberto. The
locals often carried a coral horn in their pockets which
they fingered supposedly to ward off the *iettatura,* the
evil eye, but Kinsdale had long ago decided that anyone
driving in Italy should have a rabbit's foot or its equiv-
alent.

Kinsdale turned toward the bay. A belled donkey
tethered to a newspaper kiosk shook his head at the
sports car. Houses made way for factories and ware-
houses as the bay began growing at the end of the
street. The Alfa Romeo crossed trolley and railroad
tracks and at once was confronted with a panorama
of the busiest port in Italy. Mile-long jetties reached
like spokes into the water to service cruise ships,
steamers, oilers and yachts of thirty different flags and
small, gray escort destroyers flying the colors of Italy,
France and the United States. Kinsdale headed for the
military craft and a triangular pier that jutted into the
heart of the port.

He reached a gate with the sign that read in English:

NATO
COMBINED FORCES THIRD STRATEGIC
INFORMATION GROUP

Authorized Personnel Only, was added in five languages.

A Carabiniere and an American marine stepped

out of the guardhouse to examine Kinsdale's pass and wave him through.

A two-lane road ran left to the semi-public area of the base: a Veterans' Affairs office, a community room complete with rooms for bridge playing and child care, and a commissary that sold everything from dishwashers to cereal. Kinsdale crossed that road and proceeded on a single-lane road that hid electrically armed tank mines.

Ahead were long, low bunkerlike buildings with deepset doors and air conditioning louvers for windows. A wide, concave radar spun slowly on the roof, picking up air traffic from Venice to Tunis. A radio screen pulled in satellite communications from Washington, Brussels, Casablanca, Marseilles and Tel Aviv. Below, the building sank like an inverted pyramid five stories down within a shell of rubberized, heat-proof cement capable of shouldering anything less than the direct hit of a SS-N-8 nuclear missile. There were half-a-dozen Russian submarines just outside the bay carrying SS-N-8s, and Kinsdale accepted them the way he accepted volcanos and tank mines. As part of his job.

He parked and walked energetically into the main building, flashing his pass at the two marines on guard. Glass doors slid open. He pressed his hand against the foyer's Idento-panel, which scanned his fingerprints, face and jacket ID. Inner glass doors whispered open and he strode to an elevator marked, "Authorized Persons Only—*Program Three*—Check Your Authorization."

"Take your time, the local brass isn't here yet," Mike McAllister called from the Sub-level Two coffee wagon when Kinsdale stepped out of the elevator.

McAllister was in his sixties, one of the original English cipher whizzes, short with thinning red hair. American slang was mixed with the accents of Oxford, "like an oil slick on the Thames," as Mike put it.

"It's still like D-Day minus one," General Fuller said from farther down the hall. Fuller was a man who looked as if he were designed for command. Even his private coffee mug had two stars.

"It's always D-Day minus one around here. I'll take mine black," Kinsdale moved to the wagon. One thing could be said for the Navy, they made good coffee.

"Wife and kiddies?" Mike asked.

"Fine, and you?"

Mike was a bachelor, but he shared his Naples tenement apartment with an Italian nurse half his age from the VA office.

"Not bad for a character in my advanced state of decrepitude."

"That's a long way to say dirty old man."

"John, I'm wounded," Mike grinned. "Come on, let's go have some fun. They can't start the war without us."

They raced on a pair of the Navy's most advanced Evans & Sutherland Computer Corporation display systems. Three tapes—the Monaco Grand Prix racecourse, Juan Fangio and Mario Andretti—stuttered forward and backward on the data base computer. Older display systems necessitated display file generator programs and display file software. The E & S system's complex display processor eliminated those elements to produce instantaneous simulation on a cathode ray tube. At his keyboards, Kinsdale punched in velocity, lateral direction and gear into the data bank to be filtered through the known characteristics of Andretti in

Formula-4 competition, a sum altered by fuel consumption and transmitted within real-time milliseconds onto the screen. McAllister did the same with the taped soul of Fangio, the great Argentinian.

They didn't have to wait for any printout. The E & S system was created for the simulation of a jet fighter taking off and landing on the deck of a moving aircraft carrier. Speed in three dimensions was its meat. But instead of the rolling deck of a carrier, on the display's black tube were the lines of a Grand Prix course, road, barriers, banked turns rushing at the viewer at 140 m.p.h.

"Down to the floor, Mario," Kinsdale's thumb held down the button for acceleration.

The input was interfed from one tube to another. On McAllister's display screen, the ghostly shape of the Kinsdale-Andretti racer swung in front. McAllister subtracted velocity to take advantage of the slipstream effect. The computer allowed for that, too.

"You'll overshoot, dear boy," McAllister warned, "crash through the barrier and end in flames wrapped around a concrete pylon."

"Don't you wish! This is just the hottest little driver you ever saw."

The road rolled forward. The outline of a low bridge rushed closer. McAllister tapped for acceleration.

"Got to get some sound effects into this system. Can't see you, you sneaky limey," Kinsdale complained.

"At the moment, I'm Latin. You'll see me soon enough."

They glanced back once when the door to their office opened, then went back to the action.

Janice Lowe shut the door behind her and stood with her arms crossed.

"Oh God, Fangio and Andretti at it again."

She was young and slight with soft brown hair and startling green eyes. The slightest Irish brogue touched her speech and her manner was one of easy affection. At the London Institute of War, though, she'd written a paper on "The Psychological Determinants of Soviet Strategy" that the U.S. Navy paid $80,000 for her not to publish. In her exotic specialty, she was any man's equal.

"Look out!" she cried.

Kinsdale's display disintegrated into a tangle of lines. The screen went blank and then came up, "TOTALLED."

McAllister hit the off switch triumphantly.

"He's a killer, he is. A total write-off! Fangio will have your guts for breakfast."

"Enough of this Grand Prix footwork. Next time we go to Indy."

"And I think you ran right into Princess Grace's skirts," McAllister crowed. "We should deduct some points simply for form."

"Really," Janice interrupted, "you've just reduced millions of dollars worth of complex, sophisticated electronic equipment to the status of a common pinball machine. Don't you two feel the least bit guilty?"

"Ask the loser, not me. Another go around the track, John."

"Back to work, everyone," Kinsdale ignored the taunt and stretched. "We've got a war to program."

"Make love, not war," Janice said dryly.

"Not too loud," Kinsdale warned her. "Mike will invent a game for it."

He was cut off by the metallic booming of a P.A. speaker announcing, "We are twenty-seven hours and thirty-seven minutes from Operation Hawk. All civilian and military personnel stand by for the commander's briefing at ten thirty hours."

Kinsdale glanced at his watch: 10:17. The office phone rang and Mike rolled his chair to his desk.

"Hi, Annie," he looked up at Kinsdale. "No, he's not too busy. You ought to know by now that I do all the work around here. By the way, wish Jeff a happy birthday from Uncle Mike. Tell him I'll drop off his present tomorrow. Hang on . . ." He handed the phone to Kinsdale. "Top priority call."

"All right," Kinsdale sighed into the receiver, "what did I forget now?"

"You forgot," Ann's voice said, "to tell me how much you wanted to spend for the patio. They just delivered the tiles."

"I'll leave that to you, honey. Just remember, I'm not a general."

"All right. Oh, the doorbell. That's probably the girl from the employment service. I think I'll only take her two days a week. Call me this afternoon if you get the chance. 'Bye, hon."

Kinsdale started to say goodbye, shrugged and dropped the phone.

"She hung up."

All of Sub-levels Three and Four were taken up by the deep oval of the War Room. There was a viewers' gallery. The deep middle of the room, the "pit" as the gamers called it, was a circle of IBM 2250 desk-size units. The units sucked out information from the lowest level, Sub-Five, where ranks of IBM 1130s held in waiting the laser-written magnetic tapes of data on every weapon and any arms-bearing man between Bermuda and the Indian Ocean.

A quarter of the War Room's curved wall was a display of the world. Glowing blue lines marked the Ballistic Missile Early Warning System nets around Alaska, Greenland and Britain. Blue dots marked FSS-7 and FPS-49 radars around the periphery of the United States. A cluster of blue dots formed around the giant FPS-85 phased-array radar at Eglin Air Force Base, Florida. Red lines arced around Leningrad, Yakutsk, and the East German frontier near Dresden and Nikolayev on the Black Sea. Red dots clustered at Cienfuegos Bay, Cuba.

A second great display pictured the Mediterranean from Lisbon on the west to the Black Sea on the east. Blue flotillas of the United States Sixth Fleet and the Italian and French navies were marked according to their course or anchorage. A red flotilla was pinpointed at Cairo while a second steamed through the Hellespont.

The third screen was blank. Its purpose, however, was indicated by two digital toteboards alongside it. The titles on the toteboards were MISSILES, SILOS, BOMBERS, FIGHTERS, TRANSPORT, ELIN STA, CARRIER, MISSILE CRUISER, ELIN SUB, MISSILE SUB, DESTROYER, AMPHIB, MOBILE MISSILE, TANK, PERSONNEL CARRIER, HELICOPTER, INFANTRY, and each title was above diodes that could count casualties into the millions. One board was shaded a salmon pink, the other in azure and both had bottom lines of MASS CASUALTIES and COST.

"Program Three," General Fuller proudly led the way into the pit. Trailing behind him was an international parade. Two Italian admirals, a French marshall with an entourage of colonels, two West German generals, an Israeli general in his open collar uniform, two fatigued observers from the U.S. Department of Defense and Kinsdale, McAllister and Janice Lowe.

"Very impressive," the Frenchman scanned the War Room. "Amazing technology, as always. We can count on America for that. Precisely, what is it?"

"The end, gentlemen, of error," Fuller said confidently. "But, let me put you into the whole picture. As you well know, United States Army Europe and our NATO allies were locked into one war scenario for ten years."

"Total war," one of the Germans said.

"Correct," Fuller agreed. "Total. The invasion of Western Europe by the Warsaw Pact, nuclear missiles fired between the United States and Russia, retaliatory missiles, second strike versus second strike until every major industrial and population center on each side was leveled for a century to come. Now, times have changed. Technology has developed. Aims have narrowed and, in a sense, become more dangerous."

Kinsdale had heard all of it before. He took his position at the master display unit and lit a cigaret. Mike and Janice went to their units.

"Isn't it possible American strategy has changed for neither reasons," the French marshall asked acidly. "Your new F-111 and B-1 bombers are costing you a hundred million dollars a plane. Perhaps you can't afford deep-strike warfare anymore."

Mike surreptitiously touched his keyboard. "Little frog bastard," popped up on Kinsdale's screen. Kinsdale canceled the display and stifled a laugh.

"Our strategy is not at issue today," Fuller explained. "It's theirs. Mainly their thrust around NATO's eastern flank into the Middle East and the Mediterranean. Thrusts made through political pressure and conventional arms. Thrusts far more sophisticated than all-out nuclear holocaust.

"We've tried to prepare for these thrusts with NATO

maneuvers. There was Operation Deep Furrow during which we landed American paratroopers in Greece. Operation Strong Express on Norway's northern coast, involving 300 warships, 700 aircraft and 74,000 soldiers from seven nations, the biggest NATO field maneuver in that part of the world since World War Two. Operation Alkali Canyon, where we landed 9,000 marines especially trained for Mideast combat. Operation Gallant Hand, with 25,000 soldiers exercising combat for a mid-intensity region like southern Europe."

"Staged battles driving us deeper and deeper into debt," the marshall shook his head.

"Thank you," Fuller lowered a finger on the Frenchman like a gun, "because that's my point. Program Three is the end of error and the end of waste. Right here in this War Room we can program and run more accurately a hundred strategic scenarios in the time it takes you to move one division on field maneuvers. We can tell you where every Soviet submarine is from Gibraltar to Galilee. What the Second Bulgarian Division had for breakfast today. What quality marine fuel is available for Syria. In other words, material and capability."

"But intention," the marshall reddened. "All this data. What about the human factor?"

"Janice?" Fuller turned.

Janice punched her keyboards. The third screen came alive with a hundred thousand alpha symbols arranging themselves mosaically into a portrait of a white-haired man wearing the starred cap of a Soviet admiral.

"Commander in Chief Sergei Georgievich Gorshkov," Janice spoke in a prim, flat voice, "creator of a navy that has outbuilt the United States three-to-one in the last ten years. Planner of Operation Okean, the recent Soviet sea exercise designed to seize control of the Mediterranean. A positivist who, despite Red Army opposition, argues in the Politburo for offensive strikes. A realist who knows his fleet can be bottled up at the Dardanelles and that he needs his own Mediterranean port to justify the expense of his navy. The personality profile indicates a 72 percent probability that he will attempt to gain such a Mediterranean port within the next thirty-six months."

"Where?" The Israeli spoke up for the first time.

"You, gentlemen, will decide that. You will spend the afternoon here gathering the latest data on Soviet land, air and sea capabilities. You may alter, add or subtract those capabilities by one thousand miles a day. You may create political scenarios that enhance your chances of success. You will be Admiral Gorshkov and you can pull out every stop you want. Tomorrow you will return with your strategy and play it. Misters Kinsdale and McAllister are your competition. May the best man win."

Kinsdale looked at his watch: 6:15. He'd be late for supper because the Germans kept asking for the latest updates on submerged speeds for nuclear subs.

"They'll go for a Mideast scenario, don't you think?" Mike asked wearily.

"Old hat," Kinsdale said, "besides, the logistics are wrong. They'll go for Greece."

He reached under his desk and pulled out a large gift-wrapped package. Janice took it from him and hefted it.

"It's an electronics kit."

"John!" she raised an eyebrow. "He wanted a football."

"Mike got him a football."

"But Jeff's an electronics whiz—like his father. You sure this will challenge him?"

"Ah," Kinsdale put his finger to his nose, "but the instructions are in Italian. He's a whiz, all right, but his Italian. . . ."

He took the gift back. There was a card at the bow. He wrote out, "Happy Birthday, Jeffrey. With Love from Dad."

The ride home included a worse than usual Naples traffic jam. The bus strike, Kinsdale thought. Or had the price of gasoline dropped from 1600 lira a gallon to 1500? Who could ever know? He honked along with the rest of the drivers and insinuated the Alfa Romeo through an obstacle course of bumpers.

Traffic eased along the autoroute into a seventy m.p.h. sprint, but, strangely, there was another jam as Kinsdale pulled into the housing compound gate. Tired and irritated, he leaned on his horn again until he became aware of flashing *polizia* beacons at the far end of the street.

Nothing ever happened in the compound. The residents were mainly Americans stationed in Naples for the Navy or for the branch offices of multinational companies. A little too much drinking and some discreet swinging was rumored, but nothing to bring in police.

The car inched forward. Way ahead, he could see that there were three black *polizia* sedans and two ambulances. An accident? A crowd of neighbors had gathered. He could recognize three or four of them. Their faces were pale with horror.

Concern congealed into a cold panic. Kinsdale yanked on the wheel, drove the Alfa half onto the

sidewalk and pulled the emergency brake. He emerged
and started walking. His legs moved of their own will,
each step faster than the last. Without realizing it, he
began running.

The crowd was being held back by a ring of police-
men. Kinsdale pushed his way forward until one of the
police grabbed his arm.

"In dietro, per favore!"

Kinsdale pushed the cop aside, but the cop held on.

"Lasciate libero la strada. In dietro."

"That's my house!" Kinsdale shouted in the cop's
face.

The cop let go immediately. Kinsdale could feel
around him faces filled with pity, the men mute, the
women crying. He ran between two police cars and
across the lawn. The front door was ajar. Kinsdale
knocked it open and stopped in shock.

The living room looked as if mad dogs had ripped it
apart. Chairs were on their sides, records scattered
over the floor. The sofa's padding bulged out of gashes.
Over the white carpet were wide stains of blood. Police,
seemingly in slow motion, milled around, paying no
attention to Kinsdale, asking each other, *"Qui, voglio
uno qui e qui, seriga?"* and *"Dove ispettore?"* Two
detectives tapped fingerprint powder on a banister.
Kinsdale moved past them in a daze. A bulb flashed,
illuminating a spray of blood on the wall.

Two ambulance attendants pushed by carrying a
loaded stretcher. The sheet on the stretcher was stained
at the head and middle.

"No," Kinsdale whispered.

The photographer halted the attendants, aimed his
camera and popped another bulb.

"Va bene, grazie."

Kinsdale plodded into the dining room. It was his

home but it couldn't be real. He lived here, was here at breakfast with Ann and the kids, spoke with her on the phone. This was a nightmare, unreal and grotesque. But more attendants were bringing another stretcher. The photographer was stopping it for another shot. A small child's bloodstreaked arm dangled.

Kinsdale pushed the photographer aside, grabbed the sheet and lifted it.

"Noooo!" he screamed. "No!"

Police, detectives and attendants were as still as the stains on the wall. They stared in silence, all but one older man in a suit who came out of the kitchen.

"Signor Kinsdale?"

Kinsdale rubbed his eyes as if they could be erased, as if the house and everything in it could with one act of will disappear. Knowing that he couldn't. That it was real, it was all happening.

"Signor Kinsdale," the man took Kinsdale gently by the shoulder, "please come with me."

III

Kinsdale said goodbye to his family in the morning. Their aluminum coffin cases were raised by a forklift into the side door of a USAF Stratofreighter. Kinsdale stood on the ground, a large, impassive figure in a black suit.

He'd spent the night sleeping fitfully on a bench of the morgue, insisting on staying as if, too late, he could protect them. Ann. Mark. Jeffrey. Linda.

"That's it?" a handler called from the plane's door.

"That's it. Four."

The door rolled shut. Kinsdale turned on his heel and walked towards the terminal building. A sign over the entrance said, "Arrivederci, Have a Nice Trip."

As he walked, Kinsdale slipped on a pair of sunglasses. The lenses were silvered, putting mirrors in front of his eyes.

He went home. The grass on the front yard was matted from footprints. Flashbulbs littered the sidewalk—he vaguely remembered the newspaper reporters shouting to him as the police took him away. A bicycle

—Jeff's—lay in the driveway. Kinsdale got out of the Alfa and set the bicycle back on its wheels.

Two wheels and nowhere to go. Poor old bicycle. He patted the bicycle's seat and went to the side door, and he was almost inside when he heard the bicycle's bell.

One of the neighborhood kids was by the bicycle. The boy's back was to Kinsdale, he didn't see Kinsdale returning.

"Hi, Stefano," Kinsdale patted the boy's head.

Stefano looked up, startled, and backed off a couple of steps.

"Like it?" Kinsdale knelt by the bike. The boy wavered. "Here."

Kinsdale pushed the bike gently at Stefano, who shook his head, backed off some more and, frightened, ran down the driveway.

The kitchen had the quiet air of a place ransacked and deserted. Kinsdale entered and smelled stale cigaret butts in plates, refuse of the police. Patches of fingerprint dust clung to the table and chairs. Two cups of cold coffee and rancid cream sat on the windowsill. He poured them out in the sink and deliberately went about closing cabinet doors.

In the dining room, blood was sprinkled in a wide circle around the walls. The rug was partially rolled up. The chairs were bare where swatches of stained fabric had been cut for examination. He found some coins on the floor and carefully laid them side by side on the dining table.

He noticed a dullness in his legs, but otherwise he felt he was doing pretty well.

Stuffing from the sofa covered the living room rug. Odds and ends—sports trophies, porcelain figures, books, an unopened birthday present—were dumped into cartons under the glare of a lamp that had lost its shade. An electronics kit, Kinsdale remembered, that's what he'd bought. The curtains had been torn from the windows and daylight was reflected by a small silver picture frame lying on its face. Slivers of glass fell out as he picked it up. He picked the rest of the glass out.

An Ektachrome print of Mark, Jeff and Linda leaning against each other in front of the Tower of Pisa. Out of focus and starting to tremble.

Jerkily, he set the frame on the mantel. He held his hands together until they were steady. Perfectly steady, he told himself and headed for the stairs.

The bedroom mattress was tied into a roll. The rest of the room was normal though, except for the incredible noise of his footsteps. He turned on the television and moved to the closet, slipping off his jacket.

Wrong closet. Ann's. Her dresses, her scent, all in a row. He felt the clothes as if he were trying to soothe them. A light cotton dress from Florence, her favorite for summer evenings, almost as soft as her skin. His jacket dropped to the floor and as he stooped to retrieve it he caught sight of the bureau and the bureau mirror defaced by a great smear of dried brown blood.

A sheet was rolled up with the mattress. He attacked it with his hands, swinging the whole mattress against the wall until he'd torn out a ragged square of the sheet. With the rag he rubbed the mirror, working frantically until the blood gave way to the image of a man wearing his own mirrors. A halo of blood was around his head and his cheeks were wet with tears.

"Ann. Ann, I'm sorry," he dropped his head to the bureau, "I'm sorry about everything."

His hand pulled open the top drawer. From it he took a heavy army holster and a box. The box was marked, "50 rounds, .45 cal."

He sat on the stripped bed. A soap opera was on the television. The sound was off. An overweight mother was wringing her hands and moving her mouth. Kinsdale unholstered the .45. It was wrapped in oily rags. He dropped them on the floor, revealing the long, lean automatic. The movement was still smooth. He cocked it, letting the hammer down slowly with his thumb. Satisfied, he removed the clip. From the box he gathered seven rounds and snaploaded them into the magazine. The mother was gone from the screen, replaced by a box of pasta. Kinsdale slapped the clip home into the butt. He worked the chamber back, pushing the first round into the breech. His thumb knocked down the safety. Ready.

His shoulders sagged. An ugly thing, a gun. Comes alive for only one purpose. A long, sleek snout. Crosshatched grip. Firm pull. Loaded, thirty-nine ounces of death. Ugly, but it filled a need, a deep need.

He sighed and let his head sit back on the muscles of his shoulders. With his left hand, he removed the sunglasses. He lifted the gun.

A glaze faded from Kinsdale's eyes. The television commercial was over and on the screen was a film of ambulances and a house. His house. The news was on. The same police beacons whirled. The same attendants lifted their burdens. Finally, a photograph of John Kinsdale stared from the screen at the man on the bed.

He fired. The first shot shattered the face. The .45 bucked and roared, a second time, a third and a fourth. The television set exploded with a burst of glass and the stench of short-circuited eletronics, shards and fumes filling the air like a poisonous, razor-edged cloud.

Dr. Enrico Lupo was a native Neapolitan.

Rome looked down on Naples as a pesthole of cholera, hedonism and superstition. But Naples was a thriving Greek colony called Neapolis when Rome was little more than seven hills. And Lupo bore the legacy of dark skin, a short stature with massive chest and shoulders and a near Grecian profile.

He liked his spaghetti with shellfish, wines from the slopes of Vesuvius, and the songs of *bel canto;* he distrusted foreigners. Naples always had, whether it was "liberators" from Rome, or Napoleon, or the Bourbons or the Germans. Or the Communists from Milan or the Americans from NATO.

He was not an ignorant man. As a boy he'd traveled widely and the Nazis had awarded him a scholarship in Berlin when he was still a teenager. The young Lupo studied the lithographic techniques of Dürer and returned to Naples to become the most skilled forger of German documents in southern Italy. At the end of the war and with the reorganization of Italy's police forces, he could have chosen a prestigious position with the Servizio Informazioni Difesa (SID—the intelligence arm of the government) or the Carabiniere (federal paramilitary police). Instead, he joined the municipal police because he was sick of intrigue and uniforms, and because, though he never said it aloud, he knew Naples needed him.

At sixty now, he was still robust and disdainful of private influence and spurious authority. His office, the office of the senior inspector commanding a floor of the block-long police building on Via Diaz, was the most open and efficient department in the city.

He was a very good policeman and it was a long time since he'd seen a crime as hideous as yesterday's.

"This knife," Lupo placed a hunting knife on his

desk, "was used, we know. It was found in the house. Is it yours?"

Kinsdale sat facing the senior inspector. He didn't need to take more than a glance at the weapon.

"Yes."

Lupo studied the man. Kinsdale seemed very calm, almost placid. Quite a recovery since Lupo led him from the house. The reflecting sunglasses were annoying. On the other hand, the American had not tried to hide from the preliminary inquiries behind NATO's extraterritorial status. Highly unusual for a mere computer programmer, though Kinsdale didn't seem ordinary in other ways either. No ranting, no vestige of a collapse.

"Well, we'll keep it for now," Lupo brushed the knife aside. "Would you care for some coffee?"

"No, thanks."

Lupo looked at his assistant, who stood by the door.

"Would you bring me a *caffelatte?*"

"Subito, dottore."

The assistant left and Lupo turned his full attention back to Kinsdale.

"Can you account for all your time and all phone calls you made yesterday."

Kinsdale's face tightened with anger, then he relaxed and answered softly.

"It must be very difficult for you at times." He paused. "Yes, I can."

"You are very perceptive. Yes," Lupo smiled wryly, "it's part of the job."

Damn it, the senior inspector thought, he liked the American. That made it harder.

The telephone rang.

"Excuse me." Lupo picked up the phone. *"Pronto! ... Chi c'e? ... Ah, si ... si, va bene. Me lo passi."* He cupped the phone and said to Kinsdale, "Your embassy."

Kinsdale nodded and looked out the window. The old quarter of the city, Spacca Napoli, a maze of alleys, peeling walls and iron balconies, stumbled up from the bay. He could see the cathedral. Twice a year the Feast of the Miracle of San Gennaro was held there. The blood of San Gennaro, kept dry inside the church in a flask, supposedly liquified in answer to the feast's prayers. Some miracle. Some prayers.

"Hello," Lupo spoke into the phone, "yes, Mr. Secretary, thank you, yes, very well. And yourself? . . . Good . . . How can I help? . . . Yes, of course. I have thought about that and obtained the necessary identification passes from our ministry. I think . . ." He put the phone in the crook of his shoulder and opened a manila envelope laying on the desk. Green plastic IDs spilled out. He picked one up and fingered it. "Yes, they're here already. . . . Correct, they give you full authority to . . . yes, yes, that's right. You must put the names in yourself as soon as you have nominated your investigators. . . . Not at all, Mr. Secretary, my pleasure. Goodbye."

As Lupo hung up, his assistant returned with the coffee.

"Are you sure the gentleman wouldn't have a coffee?"

"Vuoi un caffe?" Lupo asked Kinsdale again. "Do you want anything at all?"

"Nothing, thank you."

Lupo sipped from the hot cup. A strange self-confidence for a man who had lost everything, he thought. Like a machine.

"Do you have any ideas, Signor Kinsdale? Who or why?"

"None that I can think of."

"Any members of your family . . . were they ever in any kind of trouble?"

"Not to my knowledge."

"No threats?"

"No."

Lupo sat back.

"There were some tire tracks across the street from your house . . . a truck, possibly a small van."

He was leaving the house, Kinsdale remembered. Ann was waving goodbye. Something in the corner of his eye. A van, a dark van, with its hood up. Somebody leaning over the engine, maybe in a deliveryman's uniform, young, a man, longish hair, blond. Maybe red.

". . . We're checking them out. It may be that this vehicle brought the killers to your house."

"Killers, then, not a single killer," Kinsdale broke in.

"Yes," Lupo was taken back by the suddeness of the question, "to do what they did so quickly without cries for help. But a housing compound like that, there would be delivery vans all the time."

Kinsdale lapsed back into silence. Something 'was wrong, Lupo knew. He had to try a different tack.

"You have lived here for two years, Signor Kinsdale. Still, you are a foreigner here. It's possible you under-estimate us. Let me show you something that should interest you."

"All right."

Lupo led Kinsdale from the office down a hall dec-orated with tourist-variety color photos of Naples.

"You see, we have a new facility, Signor Kinsdale, one I hope will inspire your trust." The senior inspec-tor smiled. "We're even computerized. Not quite like

NATO, of course, but we are introducing new equipment almost daily."

Through double doors they entered a forensic laboratory. Technicians in white smocks were at work on a dress, coating it with luminol to bring out phosphorescent traces of blood. A blown-up photograph of a tire track occupied the attention of two more technicians. There was a high tank of water for ballistics study; a Beretta was still clamped in place after firing down into the water. Also, there were computers as Lupo claimed. Olivettis, Kinsdale noticed. Good hardware.

"Our laboratory is now considered superior to most in the United States. Our data banks alone store the magnetic images of 35,000 fingerprints and our main computer is directly linked to Interpol, which transmits new fingerprints to us by television. With the right program, our computer can take several partial fingerprints and make a whole one or, using an electronic scanner, make a smudged fingerprint into a clear one."

"Do you have any fingerprints to work on?"

"No," Lupo admitted, "but we have something else."

He led Kinsdale to a technician operating three machines in tandem.

"A gas chromatograph," Lupo pointed to a low metal cabinet, "a mass spectrometer," a tall apparatus with a face of meters, "a data bank. And this," Lupo showed Kinsdale a transparent lab envelope containing a hair, "which we found in your wife's hand. We believe it was torn from the head of her assailant. We have put a section of the hair in the chromatograph. The procedure is a complicated one."

"Dealing with molecular weight of the sample," Kinsdale said.

"Ah, yes. Correct." Lupo turned slowly to the technician. This Kinsdale was growing increasingly complicated. "Do you have the analysis chart?"

"Si, dottore. Eccola," the technician handed Lupo a sheet of paper.

Lupo skipped over the preliminary sentences concerning transfer of the evidence from a dead woman's fingers to the crime lab.

"Here. 'Microscopic analysis shows the hair to be that of a Caucasian male, between twenty-five and forty-five years of age. The pigmentation is red. Protein analysis indicates blood type A, Rh-negative. The hair is quite dirty, with traces of a lanolin hair tonic. Use of the gas chromatograph determines the composition of dirt to be thirty-six micrograms of sulfur dioxide—one hundred and ninety-nine micrograms of nitrogen.' "

"Thirty-six to one hundred and ninety-nine."

"Right," Lupo gave the paper back to the technician. "I'm sorry to put you through this, but I thought with your background . . ."

"No," Kinsdale took Lupo's hand and shook it, "thank you for doing it. You've been a great help."

As Kinsdale headed for the door, Lupo followed.

"If I want to reach you, Signor Kinsdale . . .?"

"I'll be working," Kinsdale said without looking back.

As he walked through the corridor of Sub-level Two the people he passed reacted with surprise and embarrassment. Janice Lowe was the first with the nerve to speak to him.

"We heard after you'd left yesterday. I'm so sorry, John."

"I know you are. Thank you."

"But what are you doing here? Are you all right?" she touched his arm.

"I'm O.K."

"Is there anything I can do?" There was sympathy in her green eyes, but also the professional concern of a trained psychologist. "Anything at all."

"Well, I've taken a room at the Pensione Central. I wonder if you'd mind stopping by the house tonight to pick up a few of my things . . . drop them off by the hotel."

Kinsdale gave her the key to the house.

"How much stuff?"

"Oh, a few days should be sufficient."

Mike was in the office. At the sound of Kinsdale opening the door he twisted around from the terminal.

"John!"

"Morning, Mike."

"Good to see you," he grasped Kinsdale's hand. "What can I say?" There was nothing to say. Mike grasped for words and Kinsdale could see the agony in the old man's eyes. "It's just so crazy and terrible. Look, you want to stay in my digs for a while."

"Thanks, but no."

"You're going back to the States?"

"No." Kinsdale sat at the other display unit. "The war must go on. What did the generals come up with?"

"They entered their selection at ten this morning. You were right, the Greek scenario. I was going to try to handle the program myself. . . . I mean, I knew I couldn't, but I thought you . . ."

"But now I'm back." In a businesslike manner, he pulled out a few notes. "I've made some changes in the program, too. Some different approaches."

He gave the notes to Mike. Mike scanned them

quickly, his forehead wrinkling as he went on. He looked anxiously at Kinsdale and read the notes a second time.

Kinsdale lit a cigaret, puffed and balanced the cigaret on the lip of an ashtray. Steady hands again.

"Will you help me?" he asked.

Mike set the notes down and stared at the blank eye of the display screen.

"It won't be easy, John. We've got to code it all. Paraphrase the information requests . . ."

"And if you're caught helping me . . ." Kinsdale added softly.

"I know," Mike faced Kinsdale. The silvered sunglasses hid something new and strange in his friend. But they were friends.

"Well . . . ?"

"We'd best get started," Mike said with no more hesitation.

They'd barely started when General Fuller strode into the office, a colonel tagging smartly one step behind. Mike put the notes aside. Fuller cleared his throat and laid a fatherly hand on Kinsdale's shoulder.

"You're looking fine, John, just fine."

"Thank you, General."

"John, no one, no one more than I appreciates your sense of loyalty in returning to work after . . ."

"Thank you."

"But I can't help wondering if it's the right thing. John, well," Fuller leaned down and spoke almost in a whisper, "don't you think you should try to get away for a while? Go back home?"

"What home, General?"

Fuller swallowed.

"Look, I can arrange whatever you want. A sabbatical in Hawaii? An easy tour with SEATO in Japan ... ?"

"I'd rather stay here, General."

"All right," Fuller patted Kinsdale's back, "you're a good soldier. Good to have you back. It's a Greek scenario, by the way. A pretty tricky one."

All paternal concern was gone from Fuller and replaced by relief that Kinsdale had returned. He checked his watch.

"Half an hour to wartime, men."

Fuller and his shadow exited and marched toward the War Room. He slapped his hands together. Thank God, Kinsdale had shown up, he thought. McAllister was good, but Kinsdale could make computers sing. The general himself had only a rudimentary understanding of data banks, software and magnetic tapes but he knew damn well that a good show for Program Three meant more appropriations and with more appropriations another star on his cap wasn't far behind. Janice Lowe came out of her office and walked by his side and he gave her a content hello.

"General Fuller, I'd like to talk to you about John Kinsdale."

"Certainly," he said without breaking stride.

"I'd like to program these recent events into his personal file, sir."

Fuller slowed down.

"What do you mean?"

"I think that John is far more upset than he's letting show. I want to turn his whole profile through an event probability mode."

"Look, Miss Lowe," Fuller cut her off. "I know men like Kinsdale. They're geniuses, not like us. They lead two separate lives, their machines and their families.

Let's say they're even a bit cold. They go right on without batting an eyelid. Believe me, I've just seen him. Besides, we can't run this show without him."

"I'd still like to run that profile."

"O.K., O.K., do whatever you want. Just don't interfere today."

As if on cue, the corridor of Sub-level Two echoed the voice of the loudspeaker.

"Twenty-five minutes to Operation Hawk."

IV

The gallery had a standing-room-only audience of junior officers, unseen in the low lights of the War Room. On the Command Bridge, sitting in swivel seats, were Fuller and staff officers from every NATO member nation. Technicians stood by the great display screens. In "the pit," on one side, were military programmers and the cavalcade of generals who had visited the previous day. On the other side at just two display units were McAllister and, as still as a rock, John Kinsdale.

There was a nearly fearful awe in the war theater. Operation Hawk, the acid test of Program Three, had begun with the assassination of the prime minister of Greece. Riots in Athens followed, along with a civil war between right wing factions of the Greek Army and the Greek Communist party. Kinsdale saw a lot of the influence of the French marshall in the program, a subtle viciousness that left the staff officers on the command deck silent and glum.

Kinsdale responded with C5-A transport flights to

Turkey and a shift of the Northern Army group and second Allied Tactical Air Force from the Belgian-Dutch border to Torremolinos in Spain. He didn't touch the Southern Army. He pulled USN ships ten miles out of Piraeus and called for the carrier *Saratoga* to steam north from Israel and for the carrier *Independence* to head for the Dardanelles. In light of the deteriorating situation programmed for Greece, his actions seemed weak.

Riots in Italy began, spearheaded by the Italian Communist party, which demanded no interference in Greek affairs by Italian-based NATO forces. No aid could be expected from Turkey, the NATO ally on Greece's east flank and also Greece's bitterest enemy.

SECOND DAY. 0200 HOURS. The Russian aircraft carrier *Kiev,* the pride of the Soviet Navy, steams out of the Black Sea and through the Bosporus headed for the Mediterranean with a force of two Kara-class cruisers, three SAM-carrying, Kynda-class cruisers, a Kashin-class cruiser and twenty Krivac-class frigates. Already surrounding the American fleet standing off Piraeus were fifteen Soviet submarines. A second Soviet fleet approaches from Cairo with the carrier *Moskva.*

SECOND DAY. 0300 HOURS. Blue forces arrest one hundred top Greek army officers, apparently leaving the field to Communist paramilitaries. The Greek Army abandons Athens and heads north to Thessaloniki. . . .

On the war screen, Greece was surrounded by a closing ring of Red ships. In one *coup de main,* the battle seemed over. Fuller watched disbelievingly while Kinsdale and McAllister casually stopped for refreshments from a coffee tray.

SECOND DAY. 0600 HOURS. Communists gain

control of Greek radio and announce a People's Republic and order all NATO forces fifty miles from the frontier. The radio also welcomes the fraternal aid of socialist brothers in the protection of Greek sovereignty. Over Athens fly one hundred Mig-21s and assorted Ilyushin and Takarov bombers.

Blue forces airlift two divisions of the Northern Army, destination unknown. The second Tactical Air Force also lifts off. Istanbul announces it will protect only Turkish land and sea lanes.

SECOND DAY. 0900 HOURS. The Bulgarian Army, behind a cavalry of 350 T-54 and T-62 tanks, responds to the call from Athens by pouring over the Greek border at the Stimron Pass, a deep gorge in the Orosira Mountains.

Blue forces slowly move the Greek Army up from Thessaloniki to meet the invasion.

"I can see why Admiral Gorshkov is so confident," the marshall's voice carried through the War Room.

SECOND DAY. 1000 HOURS. An incident in the Dardanelles. Turkish fishing boats are fired upon, apparently by the speeding carrier *Kiev* and its task force. The Turkish Navy responds with thirty hydrofoil missile ships, airlifted the day before on C5-As. The Dardanelles is a long and very narrow strait and the Russian task force is strung out. To the hydrofoil patrol boats, traveling at sixty knots, the big ships are sitting ducks. Struck by powerful harpoon missiles, four cruisers and five destroyers go down and the *Kiev* is foundering.

SECOND DAY. 1100 HOURS. The entire Stimron Pass is sown with tank mines by the Second Tactical Air Force on its way to the Thessaloniki air base. RAF vertical-takeoff-landing Harriers set up around the pass. Two divisions of the Northern Army parachute in front of the Bulgarians. The Northern Army has no armor; it has equipped every fourth man with TOW antitank missiles.

SECOND DAY. 1200 HOURS. The Red Air Force has set up air cover for the flotilla stalled in the Dardanelles. However, a second attack by hydrofoil patrol boats accounts for two more cruisers.

SECOND DAY. 1300 HOURS. Around the Red ring surrounding Greece a second Blue ring is growing, a ring with three ships to every one of the Red fleet. Above the Red Air Force gathers an armada of 300 Blue air superiority fighters.

SECOND DAY. 1600 HOURS. A salient of tanks has carried every land war for the past forty years. Technology has caught up. Mines, laser-guided missiles from the dodging Harriers and TOW missiles from infiltrating squads of Northern Army "tank killers" has turned the Stimron Pass into a steel graveyard. The Bulgarian Army, third in effectiveness among Warsaw Pact forces after the Russians and East Germans, trudges into a hail of personnel mines. The Greek Army, eager for vindication, moves up from Thessaloniki.

At his display panel, illuminated by its eerie blue light, Kinsdale pushed more buttons faster, moving killer Cobra helicopters into the Dardanelles, Greek tanks and artillery into the Stimron Pass, bringing one Greek division back to Athens. Figures danced on his glasses.

Other figures danced on the toteboards.

In the Red square: 1 CARRIER. 8 MISSILE CRUISERS. 6 DESTROYERS. 280 TANKS. 50 PERSONNEL CARRIERS. 23 HELICOPTERS. 2,600 INFANTRY. MASS CASUALTIES: 15,700. COST: $1,380,450,000.

In the Blue Square: 19 PATROL BOATS, 50 ATOL FIGHTERS, 300 INFANTRY, 41 HELICOPTERS. MASS CASUALTIES: 940. COST: $135,000,000.

SECOND DAY. 1610 HOURS. The carrier *Kiev* was scuttled.

SECOND DAY. 1630 HOURS. Under Blue air cover, a division of the Greek Army landed at Athens.

SECOND DAY. 1700 HOURS. The one-day government of the People's Republic of Greece arrived by motor launch onto the carrier *Moskva*, which retreats from the Greek coast escorted by two hydrofoil patrol boats of the Italian Navy.

"DATA NOW SHOWS NO CAPABILITY OR INTENT OF RED FORCES TO CARRY ON GAMES," flashed on the war screen.

"Congratulations, Wellington," Kinsdale turned in his seat to McAllister. "You've won."

Across the pit, the marshall leaned disbelievingly over his display unit. On the Command Bridge, General Fuller slapped an Italian admiral on the knee.

"Bravo, bravo, Joe," Fuller beamed magnanimously, "Your people did real well. And, Mustapha," he reached back to shake hands with the Turkish observer, "super, just super."

The "losing side" swarmed across the pit to congratulate Mike and Kinsdale. Enthusiastic applause filled the gallery.

"Log it up, Bill," Fuller told his aide. "In under twenty-five hours, game time, Operation Hawk successfully countered. Enemy forces decimated and in retreat, minimal damage to Allied Forces. That's it," he laughed loudly, "the war's over."

Kinsdale cleaned up his desk. He looked up to see

Janice watching him thoughtfully. The marshall stepped between them.

"Masterful work, Mister Kinsdale. The daring was what I hadn't expected. Tell me, that incident in the Dardanelles, who fired on the fishing boats?"

Kinsdale smiled.

"I thought so," the marshall nodded. "If ever you desire to live in Paris, let me know. A man with your talents can be accommodated."

"Top notch, John, top notch," Fuller passed by with a pat on the back. "There's going to be some champagne popping in the VIP lounge. Come on by if you get the chance. You too, Mike."

The generals filed out to their celebratory drinks. The technicians wrapped up printouts and carted them off for analysis. Janice was the last to leave Kinsdale and Mike alone in the vast emptiness of the War Room.

Kinsdale looked at the glowing toteboards. Mass casualties. Cost. Victory.

"I had a feeling you wanted to get at the computer," Mike said, "so I scuttled the *Kiev* a little ahead of schedule."

"You made the general's day."

"Keep the customers happy." Mike's smile slipped off his face. From his pocket he fished the note Kinsdale had given him earlier. "You want to go through with this?" Kinsdale only waited, his hands over the plastic buttons of his dark display unit. "Very well, John," Mike sighed. "Just what is thirty-six micrograms of sulfur dioxide and one hundred and ninety-nine milligrams of nitrogen?"

"An extraneous set of chemicals collected from somebody's hair."

"Somebody?"

"It could be from a factory, could be part hair lotion. Who could I ask?"

"U.S. Bureau of Standards would keep records of most American and foreign hair solutions. The Environmental Protection Agency would have breakdowns of factory and car emissions."

"We still have telelink circuits open to the States?"

"Linked to the National Intelligence Switching System," Mike flicked his unit's OPEN switch. Kinsdale followed suit. Their display units came alive with the blue pulsing of electron guns waiting for a command.

"We'll interrogate Bureau of Standards, EPA and the Massachusetts Institute of Technology," Kinsdale said. "Go out parallel and hook their data processors up to us here."

"What about telephone numbers?"

"Watch."

Kinsdale picked up the unit's telephone receiver and set it on an amplifier cradle. He dialed. In a second, a voice responded from the amplifier.

"Washington Information."

"Operator, this is ATS Central. We're running a test. Give me a line to your National Electronic Listing System."

"That's Bethesda. Where are you calling from?"

"Washington, D.C.," Kinsdale said.

"I'll put you through."

Impulses, that was all. Kinsdale's voice instantly broken by Program Three's 1150s into high-speed radio signals, which were transmitted to an orbiting ELIN satellite and broadcast into the National Electronic Switching System with less effort than dropping a dime into a pay phone on Pennsylvania Avenue. His display amplifier buzzed and answered.

"This is directory test circuit, insert your key codes.
. . . This is directory test circuit, insert your key
codes. . . ."

"You know the codes?" Mike asked.

"I should," Kinsdale began typing, "I programmed
them."

In place of the recorded voice came a discreet series
of electronic beeps.

"We're hooked in, Mike. Just type the name and
address into the terminal. Program Three will search
for the number and dial it."

"Nice."

Below the War Room, in the humidified galley of
fourth-generation 1130 computers, two machines
moved with an animated stutter, file reels jerking magnetic tape back and forth through capstans. The mes-
sages Kinsdale and Mike typed out were translated
into Fortran, a language of mathematical equations. In
Virginia and Massachusetts, other computers awoke
to the call of Fortran. Their tapes joined in a chorus.
Light beams played over laser-written reels. A laser
memory process system could write a 5,000-word
dossier for 200 million Americans on a single, 4,800-
foot reel of one-inch computer tape.

It didn't take long for the answer to come, spelled
out across the War Game screen.

"The air in the city of New York. Analysis indicates
composition of mean atmosphere of the Greater New
York Metropolitan area."

"Checked?" Kinsdale asked.

"Confirmed," Mike saw a second readout appear on
his display.

"New York, then," Kinsdale canceled the War
Game screen. "Somebody who recently came from

New York. How would I find a white, redheaded male, twenty-five to forty-five years old, blood type A, Rh-negative, who left New York for Italy in the last few days?"

"State Department. Passports for all redheaded male passport carriers. If he's American, we could check Selective Service for type A, Rh-negatives and cross check. If he's alien, they'll have all that information at Immigration. When we have a short list we transfer that to JFK International, Boston and Washington for departure records. When you say 'a few days' how many do you mean?"

"Depends on how often he washes his hair. Say three days . . . no, make it five."

"The age again," Mike began typing.

"Between twenty-five and forty-five."

Kinsdale lit a cigaret. Before the smoke of his match cleared, an answer danced on the War Game screen.

"Two Caucasian males, red hair, blood type A, Rh-negative, American nationals. Alexander Taylor, twenty-seven, embarked JFK INT May 8, arrived Rome May 9. Edward Fonseca, forty-four, embarked JFK INT May 10, arrived Rome May 11."

"Do you want passport numbers, John?"

"Store them. Photos, get me photos."

The words broke into alpha symbols, which re-assembled themselves on either side of the screen into light and dark and then into face-front passport photos. Poor quality, the fault of the photographer, not the screen. Expressionless faces, neither with the longish hair Kinsdale was looking for.

"Track their movements on your display, Mike."

"I already have. Alexander Taylor, May 9, Excelsior Hotel in Rome. Rented a Fiat 611 from Hertz, checked out on May 12. No record since, which is rather unusual for an American tourist unless he's with friends or living in the park.

"Edward Fonseca, May 11, 12, 13, International Hotel, Rome. Then, Majestic Hotel, Naples, May 14, 15, 16. . . ."

Meanwhile, in the cool galley below the pit, a third computer had come alive, sending data not to the War Room but to the office of Janice Lowe.

On the display screen in her office a different and far more complete history was rolling:

JOHN MILTON KINSDALE

BORN TULSA, OKLA., JAN. 3, 1930.

FATHER MILTON KINSDALE AND MOTHER MARY KINSDALE DIED CAR ACCIDENT 1932.

SUBJECT PLACED IN CHARITABLE INSTITUTIONS FROM WHICH HE ESCAPED REGULARLY AND WHERE HE WAS RATED INCORRIGIBLY DANGEROUS.

ENLISTED U.S. ARMY 1947, TRAINED AS RADIO TECHNICIAN. SUBJECT GIVEN SERGEANT GRADE 1949, GRADE OF 2ND LIEUT. 1950.

SERVED IN KOREAN ACTION 1950-52 AS SQUAD LEADER OF RADIO TRANSMISSION INTELL. OPERATION BEHIND ENEMY LINES. AWARDED SILVER STAR, TWO PURPLE HEARTS.

SERVED FORT DIX, N.J., AS INSTRUCTOR IN UNARMED COMBAT AND ELECTRONIC INFORMATION GATHERING, 1953.

SERVED FORT HOOD, TEX., 1954, DESIGNING FIELD RADIO TRANSMITTERS. GRADE OF CAPTAIN. DEMOB. 1955

ENROLLED MASS. INST. OF TECH. 1955. BSC 1957.

ENROLLED CAL. INST. OF TECH. 1957. MSC 1958. MASTER THESIS ON COMPUTER CODING FOR AIRCRAFT RADAR. CLASSIFIED.

ENROLLED CAL. INST. OF TECH. 1958. DSC 1959. DOCTORATE ON FUTURE OF FIELD COMPUTERS FOR TACTICAL COMBAT. TOP SECRET AND CLASSIFIED.

MARRIED ANN BOOKER 1960. (SON MARK MILTON 1961, SON JEFFREY ALLEN 1964, DAUGHTER LINDA BOOKER 1969)

EMPLOYED INTERNATIONAL BUSINESS MA-CHINES, ARMONK, N.Y., 1960 TO 1970, AS RE-SEARCH TEAM LEADER IN DEVELOPMENT OF LASER AND MICROWAVE TECHNOLOGY.

EMPLOYED DEPARTMENT OF DEFENSE 1971 AT CIVIL SERVICE GRADE 15. ASSIGNED WASH., D.C., LED RESEARCH OF COMPUTER CODING OF D.O.D. SATELLITE PROGRAM, RE-SEARCH OF STRATEGIC COMBAT INTELLI-GENCE GATHERING.

ASSIGNED NAPLES 1974. RESEARCH CHIEF OF NATO PROGRAM THREE WAR GAME THEATER....

PSYCHOLOGICAL PROFILE: SUBJECT IS PER-FECT TEAM LEADER, POSSESSING SELF-CONFIDENCE, HIGH INTELLIGENCE AND AGGRESSIVENESS. HE HAS PROGRESSED FROM A BACKGROUND OF EMOTIONAL DE-PRIVATION AND HOSTILITY.

EVENT INPUT: MURDER OF ANN, MARK, JEFFREY AND LINDA KINSDALE.

REANALYSIS: SUBJECT IS, IN ESSENCE, A

COMBAT TEAM LEADER. HIS BASIC MAKEUP OF EMOTIONAL DEPRIVATION AND HOSTILITY IS AWAKENED WITH TOTAL LOSS OF NEW LIFE HE HAS MADE.

EVENT PROBABILITY MODE: SUBJECT WILL ATTEMPT RETALIATION AGAINST INDIVIDUALS RESPONSIBLE FOR HIS FAMILY'S MURDER— 94 PERCENT.

EVENT PROBABILITY MODE: SUBJECT WILL SUCCEED IN RETALIATION AGAINST SUCH INDIVIDUALS—68 PERCENT.

V

A tourist bus with the English slogan "You Deserve Your Vacation" painted below sightseeing windows was parked beside the main entrance to the excavations of Pompeii. Parked behind the bus was an Alfa Romeo.

Pompeii had once been a different kind of vacation spot. Emperors and courtesans and poets holidayed there, made love on high, plush beds, worshiped the gods Isis and Mercury and sweated off their hangovers in the Stabian Baths. Now, where the crust of hardened lava had been cut away, gum wrappers lay in Roman gutters. Under the bed of a long dead prostitute was an empty Kodak box. Scrawled across an ancient mural was, "Vota Communista!"

The bus's tour group wandered—Americans with Instamatics, Germans with Leicas and Japanese with Nikons—around the exhumed Forum. One redheaded man kept urging his wife to stand closer to a headless statue of Venus.

"See if you can put your arm around her, Agnes.

What's the matter . . . damn."

"You've got the lens cap on, Eddie."

"Oh, yeah. That's better."

"Hurry up, hon. I keep getting my heels caught in these silly stones."

"That's fabulous. Great, just hold it. What?" The man wheeled around at the tap on his shoulder.

Kinsdale loomed over the redheaded man. Kinsdale's jacket was unbuttoned; if the man made another sudden move, Kinsdale would go for the automatic without asking questions.

"Is your name Fonseca?"

"Yeah . . . Eddie Fonseca." He paused. "Oh, you must be with the charter flight people. They said on the bus you'd try to meet us here. Agnes! It's the charter flight man!"

The woman hobbled towards them.

"I thought you guys were going to stand behind us," Fonseca pointed angrily at Kinsdale. "We can't afford these new prices. That room last night was supposed to be included, but the guy at the desk made me pay almost double."

"I'm not with your tour." Kinsdale flashed the card he'd stolen from Lupo's office. "I'm with the American consulate."

"Oh?" Fonseca's anger melted into apprehension. "What's wrong?"

"Are you from New York City?"

"Now, now, wait a minute," Fonseca put his hand up.

"Let me explain," Agnes Fonseca cut in. She wore a drip-dry pink dress that sagged in the air's humidity. Anxiously, she wrung her hands. "It's all my fault. Eddie thought that I had already registered the necessary three months in advance . . ."

". . . But the man at the tour office said it would be
O.K.," Fonseca picked up. "Said it was just a technicality, right, Agnes."

"Eddie's right, sir."

"You don't live in New York City?"

"Nope. New Haven . . ."

"Another technicality," Agnes dropped her head
guiltily.

"Agnes, for Christ's sake!"

"I'm sorry, Eddie. But I told you I didn't feel comfortable doing it this way. It's just not right. It's
cheating . . ."

Fonseca reddened. Beads of sweat popped out on
his upper lip and temples. Along the redheaded man's
hairline was something Kinsdale had never anticipated.
A faint network of lace wilting in the heat of the day.

"Agnes, we're not going to spend the rest of our
lives behind bars because we ignored two membership
technicalities! Besides, they took our money and
they're giving us crummy service to boot. If anybody
gets in trouble, it's them. Right, mister?"

They turned to Kinsdale, but he was gone. And at
the headless statue, a doughty Japanese wife was
posing for her husband.

"A freak occurrence. At least, let us hope so,"
Lupo told the three Americans sitting across from his
desk.

Americans, to the trained eye, always looked more
alike than different. Their suits were good quality
ready-made, something impossible in Italy where
"ready-made" meant "poor" and most men had their
suits done by tailors. Their shoes were of different

widths; in Italy there were many sizes, but only one width. They were beefy, well-nourished and pleased. The men Lupo had met from the Central Intelligence Agency had another characteristic in common, a smooth, assured arrogance.

He opened a manila envelope and passed out three green plastic cards.

"These will help you circulate more freely. They have been signed by the Minister of the Interior. If anyone questions your authority—which occasionally does happen here—just have them call the telephone number at the bottom of the card and one of my people will authenticate you."

The CIA men looked at their passes as dubiously as if they held tickets to Disneyland.

"I appreciate very much your government's aid in this investigation," Lupo said.

The senior agent was a man named Morrisey. He attached a pained expression to his face.

"Well, when one of our nationals gets hit, we all feel it, Inspector."

"True. Everyone feels it," Lupo emphasized. "I can recommend some hotels or restaurants, if you're interested."

"I told them," Morrisey gestured to the two other agents, "Naples is the home of the pizza. I just hope all my Italian hasn't disappeared in the last ten years."

"You'll find merely making the effort to communicate in Italian will endear you to my countrymen. Just try not to use your hands too much."

The agents laughed. Too easily, Lupo thought. As if their visit were some social call to exchange business cards.

"Let's pray," Lupo said, "that this is not political,

gentlemen. At the moment, our government, like yours, needs less, not more cause for anxiety. Let's pray the Kinsdale massacre is an isolated case."

"Inspector," Morrisey leaned forward, "anything we know, you'll know. A totally frank exchange of information, you can count on that."

Kinsdale had returned to the War Room. He sat at his display staring at the game screen on the wall.

Half of the screen was a map of Italy, Rome and Naples marked by stars. On the other half of the screen was the face of Alexander Taylor. A different kind of map. Casually handsome but with a thin, hypertense mouth. Dark eyes staring at innocent children, or only startled by the passport photographer's flash. A thin forehead and a patrician's long nose. Were they signs pointing of viciousness and insanity, or sensitivity? He had red hair, but not long. Combed tightly back. Another Fonseca, another dead end?

He became aware of another person in the War Room and turned wearily to the smile of Janice Lowe.

"Oh, hi, Janice. Didn't hear you come in."

"Playing with road maps now?" she looked at the game screen.

"Umm, that's nothing." His thumb casually hit CANCEL. The game screen went blank. "Sit down. Give me a nice Irish reprimand for playing pinball with the computers again."

She sat on the edge of the display unit. A pretty girl, Kinsdale thought. Sweet and brilliant at the same time. Some navy captains had tried making time with her, with no luck. Their loss, he figured.

"Just like Las Vegas," she said softly.

"Odds are better."

Her eyes traveled over the always glowing world map on the War Room wall. Blue radar fences against red radar walls. Missile poised against missile, army against army, waiting for the next round, a new scenario. But the toteboards showed that a war had already begun. In the Blue square under MASS CASU-ALTIES was the number four. Kinsdale had forgotten to erase that.

"You ever get into soft data, John? Into psychological data?"

"No." Kinsdale looked at the keys of his unit. "Never got into that stuff. What was the name of that place you worked at?"

"The Bay Institute."

"Huh. Does the behavioral science section give reasonable odds?"

"Yes, we do. John, I threw your chart in yesterday. That's what I came to talk to you about."

He sipped from a cup of lukewarm coffee.

"I hope I didn't bore you."

"No." Janice reached out and touched his arm. "You frightened me."

"There's a monster in our midst," he smiled.

"John . . . I want to help you."

He set the cup down. There was no more smile.

"I know what you're doing, John. I want to help you. But you have to stop this . . . this . . ."

"What?"

"Retaliation. Revenge. Stop everything to do with war games. We'll go into analysis and therapy. Continue this vendetta and you'll lose. . . ."

"Lose what? Nothing. See," he became excited, "this is the beauty of it. I have nothing to lose. I can't sustain any losses, then. Everything is in my favor. You see that, don't you?"

"No!"

He rubbed his face.

"This chart you ran. Did you tell General Fuller about it?"

"Not yet."

"I'm asking you, I'm begging you, Janice. Don't show it to him. Please."

She shook her head.

"John, oh, John."

"Please. This one thing for me."

Janice wiped her eyes and when she spoke her voice was cracking.

"All right. If you promise me, John. One condition, that you don't take any unreasonable chances."

"A promise. No unreasonable chances," he agreed.

Eddie and Agnes Fonseca were coming out of their hotel when they were met by a distinguished looking Italian, who took each of them by the arm and led them to a police car parked at the curb. The Fonsecas exchanged frightened glances.

"Signor Fonseca?" Lupo asked.

"Uh, yeah," Fonseca said after a moment's thought, "that's right." He looked into the back of the car, where two officers sat with guns on their laps.

"A question. You came directly from Rome to Naples?"

The inspector knew the answer, which had come out of the computer room fifteen minutes before.

"Yes sir. You see, uh, my wife's parents used to live near Naples and . . ."

". . . We wanted to discover our roots," Agnes Fonseca jumped in.

"And," Lupo asked dryly, "have you been successful?"

"Well . . ."

"May I ask you a personal question, Signor Fonseca?"

"Sure . . . shoot," Fonseca blurted out.

"You'll pardon me, but when is the last time you washed your hair?"

"Huh?"

"Your hair, Signor. Did you wash it in Rome?"

"Well, no. You see, I, uh, wear a toupee. A hairpiece."

Lupo let out a long exhale, touching his brow and mouth with more than a little embarrassment.

"Look," the American couldn't restrain himself. The rooms, the missing tour representative, nothing had gone right. "Was that one of your men yesterday? I feel like I'm being accused of . . ."

"There was a man yesterday?" Lupo put his hand on Fonseca's chest.

"Well . . . yeah. He kind of scared . . . Agnes, here."

"What did this man look like?"

"Oh. Tall. Whitish hair. And these damn sunglasses, you know, the kind that reflect everything. A real bully."

"And very good-looking, I thought," Agnes added.

"An American?" Lupo asked. "Did he give you a name?"

"No," Fonseca turned from glaring at his wife. "Said he was with the American consulate. He flashed some green card."

"Thank you, Signor Fonseca," Lupo said quietly. He looked out toward the bay. "I was wondering where a certain card went."

*   *   *

That evening, 250 kilometers north of the Bay of Naples, a delivery van rolled through the Roman suburb called EUR. It was to have been Mussolini's world's fair, instead the grounds had become one of the capital's most modern and exclusive neighborhoods. Highrise condominiums rose stark and white in the glare of street lamps. A line of well-dressed moviegoers waited outside a cinema showing *The Sting*. The van's driver, a young man with longish red hair, drove slowly by, attracting no attention. At his side was a pretty, blonde girl with the fresh, scrubbed face of the American Midwest. She examined herself in her compact, then put it in her purse, tucking the "Cover Girl" under a lightweight Beretta 950-B automatic.

Curtains were drawn over the window of the rear of the van. An occasional shaft of light stole in to slide over six quiet figures. They sat on rough benches, each man holding an automatic rifle, a recoil-operated, 7.62 mm. G-3, the standard NATO weapon. The perfect irony so far as the men were concerned.

The van left EUR for an even more exclusive area of private villas. Renaissance villas with ornate iron gates. Ultra-modern villas in the shape of geodesic domes.

The girl in front checked an address and pointed down the road. The van turned onto a private lane bordered by shrubs and poplars. The lane led to an expansive nineteenth-century villa with landscaped grounds and into a cobbled courtyard beside the villa's kitchen door. The sound of Frank Sinatra came from the living room's bright windows.

The girl rang the doorbell.

Mrs. Penny Simpson put away a dish towel and

looked through the kitchen window. One couldn't be too careful. There were all those kidnappings going on, not to mention that terrible incident down in Naples a few days ago. She was reassured by the sight of the girl outside. Long, bright hair, casually dressed but clean, and plainly an American. Mrs. Simpson unlocked the door.

"Yes?"

"Are you Mrs. Simpson?" the girl asked eagerly. "I'm Pidgeon."

"Oh, yes. You're the girl who called about taking care of the children. It's a little late now."

"I'm sorry. May I come in?"

"Certainly. The children are in bed now, but I know my husband would like to . . ."

Pidgeon moved quickly inside the kitchen. As Mrs. Simpson started to close the door, Pidgeon pressed the Beretta at the woman's ear.

"Don't close the door, Mrs. Simpson."

Mrs. Simpson watched the back of the van open and the men leaping out with their weapons.

A cellophane package of peanuts dropped into the vending machine's tray. Kinsdale picked up the package and leaned against the wall. Supper. Peanuts and a coke. With the salt of complete frustration.

"John!"

Mike had popped into the hall from their office.

"Come here," he waved. "I think I'm onto something."

When Kinsdale arrived, Mike was back at one of the office display units. The unit's PRINTOUT was activated and a paper tape lay curled on the desk.

"We're still using the National Intelligence Switching System as our primary telelink," Mike said. "This is weird. They're transmitting to a lot of stations that aren't normally on their network."

Kinsdale figured the tape. Algebraic symbols, dots and dashes ran the length of the paper.

"It's in code."

"Correct. A spin-off of the 17/14 LCD codes. I've just run it through our standard cryptology program. No sweat."

"So what have we got?" Kinsdale asked impatiently.

Mike hit the console's DISPLAY switch. As the screen began to glow, he hit REPEAT. The glow shaped itself into words:

THE SECOND THREE-DAY ULTIMATUM EX-PIRES TONIGHT 2400 HOURS — IN THE EVENT OF ANY INCIDENT — DETERMINE LINK — HOWEVER TENUOUS — TO KINSDALE FAM-ILY — *STOP* — YOU ARE DIRECTED TO PRO-CEED WITH UTMOST DISCRETION — AND LOWEST PROFILE — *STOP* — INSURE DOWN-GRADE PRESS COVERAGE.

"Ultimatum?" Kinsdale exploded. "From whom, for what?"

"John ..."

"This means, this means there was a first ultimatum. Before Ann . . . before my family was hit. An ultimatum we never heard about. And now this goddamn message has probably been rolling all day while I've been beating my head against a stone wall."

"John, if there's a reaction to this message, we'll know soon enough." Mike hit CLEAR; the screen went blank, waiting. "I don't know what, but something related to you, to what we're after is supposed to happen, *was* supposed to happen before midnight."

Kinsdale's eyes swept up to the wall clock: 12:15.

A tape began chattering from the side of the console. Simultaneously, the message appeared on the display.

The first word was: "ROME ..."

VI

The blue police beam rolled over ambulance, police
car, a knot of waiting attendants, windows, the kitchen
door of the Simpson villa, police, a broken window and
bloodstained curtain, another ambulance, police car,
forensic van and an Alfa Romeo coming to a stop. A
tall man wearing sunglasses in spite of the dark got out
of the Alfa. A uniformed policeman looked at his pass
and let him through.

The same, Kinsdale thought. Same shouted orders in
Italian. Same flash of bulbs through the window, attendants waiting to carry away their limp cargo. Same
nausea that made the feet feel like lead.

Two black Fords were parked off to the side. One
was empty. In the other, a man sat with the door open
while he talked in the phone of the car's transmitter.

"Roger your last Able Baker. I'll be here until the
locals finish up."

As he approached, Kinsdale heard an incomprehen-
sible crackle from the radio.

"Check, every assistance. Sure. Yeah ... O.K., right, over and out."

The man sat back with a sigh. He looked up at Kinsdale and Kinsdale's stolen pass.

"I'm from Naples," Kinsdale put the card away.

The man looked at the house blankly. He was middle-aged, hair receding, dark circles under the eyes.

"Naples? Why not? Let's have a circus. There are already four CIA men from Rome inside." He looked at his watch. "Two-thirty. You must have jets on your car. Well, some people will bust their balls to get a piece of the action, I guess. No offense," he offered Kinsdale a tight smile. "George Edmonds at your service. I'm with the embassy."

Kinsdale leaned on the car fender.

"What happened?"

"Nothing much. Five dead—two adults, three minors. American citizens. One victim: trauma incurred by cranial fracture due to fire arm projectile. Three victims: massive hemorrhage of internal organs ... knife wounds. Brian Simpson, aged two, death by . . ." Edmonds took a deep breath, ". . . by strangulation. What else is there to know, Mister?"

"All the details," Kinsdale said coldly. "Everything."

"Then you trot your ass in there and get them, damn it," Edmonds half-rose from the car seat. "You're the cop. I'm just a crummy rubber stamp foreign service employee. The details? Dead kids. Bill Simpson. Penny Simpson. They're . . . they were friends of mine. My house is the nearest one to here. Well, maybe you're used to this. This is your job. Do you have any idea what it's like to see your best friends stiff as boards with their blood and guts spilled over their house?"

Behind his glasses, Kinsdale blinked.

"Take it easy . . ."

"Take it easy, take it easy—that's all I ever hear. How long are we going to take this . . . this. . . . Look!"

Edmonds pointed at a pair of ambulance attendants who were sharing a smoke and laughing. One executed a fake soccer kick.

"Come on, tell me. You're 'The Man,'" Edmonds looked up at Kinsdale. "That poor bastard in Naples, and now Bill. You know what he did in the embassy? Liaison with WHO, the World Health Organization. He handed out food to starving people. Made sure it got to them. He wasn't some fatcat millionaire, some secret agent, but . . . he was American."

"That's right."

"That's what, six American kids. That's right for sure. Aren't you getting tired of having your ass kicked by these punks?" Edmonds' voice rose.

"Keep it down."

"What for? I think people should know what the hell's going on!"

Kinsdale reached in the car and twisted Edmonds' collar tight around his neck.

"Shut up. Shut up or you're in trouble."

Kinsdale looked around. None of the Italians had heard the shouting above the wail of a newly arrived ambulance. Edmonds, tears in his eyes, offered no resistance to Kinsdale's grip.

"So sue me," the foreign service officer said levelly.

Kinsdale let go. Edmonds brushed his wrinkled collar with some dignity. The car radio squawked.

"Excuse me," Edmonds picked up the receiver. "Roger Able Baker . . . O.K., will do. In the morning, right? . . . No, I've got company . . ."

Kinsdale shook his head urgently and put a finger to his lips. Edmonds frowned.

". . . No . . . I said I'd like some company. It's getting late . . . O.K., Able Baker, see you tomorrow. Over and out."

He hung up and regarded Kinsdale with disbelief.

"You people are too much, you know that. We're going to keep our own people in the dark?"

"Aren't we already?"

Edmonds paused. Maybe the dark circles had grown under the foreign service officer's eyes in one night, Kinsdale thought. There was a sharp new glint in them now.

"I don't want anyone to know I'm here," Kinsdale took a chance. He had to sooner or later. "They want to play this like an isolated incident. That's not it, not it at all."

Edmonds started to answer, then reconsidered. He rubbed his eyes.

"Christ, I need a drink."

Their attention was taken by activity at the Simpson kitchen door. The attendants were emerging with their burdens. The first stretcher held something pitifully small.

"Why the kids, damn it?" Edmonds asked. "Why them?"

"I don't know," Kinsdale shut his eyes.

"Hey, what's your name, again?" Edmonds got out of the car and stood up; he wasn't going to be sitting when his friends were taken by.

"Evans."

"I mean like Frank, Sam, George . . . what do people call you?"

"Frank. Frank Evans."

"Maybe I misread you, Frank."

Kinsdale turned away from the ambulances.

"Let's get that drink together," he suggested.

The Disco Nero stayed open all night a block from the Spanish Steps. Edmonds chose it; the discotheque was a short walk from the embassy. A mirrored ball, that kind that had been retired from American dance floors in the thirties, spewed colored lights over gyrating kids. The latest Italian imitation of the Rolling Stones bellowed from five-foot speakers. Edmonds and Kinsdale sat at the bar, each with a martini.

"Can you believe it, Frank. I helped liberate this city. Yeah. And I thought that was going to be the greatest moment in my life. Sure. No more Duce, no more war, Americans and Italians brothers forevermore. Oh, how they loved us then, Frank buddy. Us and the buck. I sure have learned a lot since then."

Two dancers, a Roman boy and girl each about twenty, perched on the stools next to Kinsdale. They listened, smirking at Edmonds.

". . . Better if every American had his throat cut," the boy said deliberately loud enough to be heard over the cacophony. The girl giggled. He reached for his drink and found his wrist in Kinsdale's grasp.

"Do you know what it feels like?" Kinsdale asked smoothly.

"What feels like?" the boy's sneer was wearing thin. He tried to pull loose or raise his drink, but he couldn't budge Kinsdale's hand.

"To have your throat cut."

"I wouldn't know," the boy swallowed.

Kinsdale snapped the boy's hand sideways. The glass cracked on the bar, spilling campari and coming up with a jagged edge.

"Americans bleed. Maybe you don't bleed," Kinsdale wondered.

The boy's eyes rotated downwards as he watched the glass in his hand being forced under his chin. Kinsdale's other arm went in a friendly fashion around the boy's shoulders, forcing him forward. The girl watched in horror. At the last moment, Kinsdale relaxed his grip and the glass dropped down the boy's chest, spoiling his silk shirt.

"Dance," Kinsdale advised him, "and keep dancing."

Edmonds and Kinsdale moved to a booth at the urging of the bartender.

"Due martini ancora, per favore," Kinsdale told the waiter.

"Here's to you," Edmonds raised the dregs of his first drink, "and here's hoping you nail all those buggers and all the dirt like them right to the wall."

"Sounds like you know who they are."

"What they are. Frank, old buddy, I am an old foreign service hand. Nothing, and I mean nothing, goes on that I don't eventually know about."

"Not the way this stuff is being played, George," Kinsdale shook his head. "No offense, as you say, but you don't know balls about bingo this time. No way."

Their second round arrived. Edmonds downed half his new drink in one gulp and leaned over the table unsteadily.

"Don't come on strong with me, Mr. CID. I know you super cops like to hog the information market, but let me tell you something. There's a lot of people like me, people in sensitive spots, who wheel and deal with a lot of U.S. and Italian agencies. Christ, we should work together, not everyone in his own little compartment. We have to before we have more . . . statistics. Waiter! Another round. Doubles."

He ran his finger around the rim of his glass.

"That little kid . . . the Simpson kid. Used to bike over to my place. I haven't got family, he just came over to see me. I kept peanut butter and jelly around for sandwiches. See, he liked me. A nice boy . . ."

"All right," Kinsdale didn't want to hear anymore about nice boys. Nice boys were victims. He was interested in predators. "Maybe you can add something. What do people like you come across?"

Edmonds began. With a rush of bitterness, disgust and martinis three through six, he described the duties of a diplomatic professional. For sixty minutes, Kinsdale listened, supplying nothing more than an occasional "yes" or "no" and a signal to the waiter for more liquor. As Edmonds slipped into martini number seven, Kinsdale excused himself and went to the bar to buy a token for the phone.

The pay phone, with a smudged half-shell of Plexiglas to keep out 50,000 decibels of rock, was by the cloakroom. He could keep an eye on Edmonds through the bar mirror.

"Combined Forces," an instant answer came to his dial.

"Program Three," Kinsdale asked.

Coded beeps started singing. Then, in Naples, a phone rang. Twice, three times. Mike would be asleep at his console. Maybe his nurse had come by with a blanket and a goodnight kiss. Kinsdale hoped so for the old boy's sake. Six rings.

"McAllister," Mike came onto the phone.

"It's John."

"Where are you?"

Kinsdale glanced at the bar mirror. Edmonds was slumped in the booth, staring moodily at his drink.

"Never mind where, just listen," Kinsdale directed.

"In April a letter was received in Washington, addressed to the president of the United States. It had an Italian postmark. Substantially, this is what it said. On May 16, an American family residing in the Mediterranean area would be destroyed. The family would be picked at random. After that, one more family would be destroyed every two days until their demands were met."

"What demands?" Mike asked after a painful moment.

"The release of political prisoners in western Europe. And ten million dollars from the U.S."

"What prisoners?"

"They cover a pretty wide spectrum of political tourists. Arabs, Irish, Basques, you name it."

"Then why pick on Americans?"

"I guess they think we've got the money and the muscle to lean on our allies. Or maybe they just want to humiliate us."

"Any idea who 'they' are?"

"None. The letter was made up of words cut from the *International Herald Tribune*. American families weren't alerted because no one wanted to start a panic, and because the letter wasn't taken seriously. Not until a few days ago. Now, just about every U.S. agency is involved in this thing and they're all operating independently. I want a list of all suspected terrorists and their cells in Europe, regardless of their affiliation."

"John, you're asking for a list of fifty thousand names."

"What else can I do?"

Kinsdale hung onto the phone. After a pause, Mike answered.

"Can you get near a terminal so we can link up?"

"I'll try. Can you stay put there tomorrow?"

"Yes. The general thinks I'm working overtime on a new program for the capture of Prague. He's an innocent chap in his way."

"Talk to you tomorrow."

"John, take care."

The Simpson villa hadn't received its last visitor of the night. Dr. Enrico Lupo, rumpled from his ride from Naples, walked around the courtyard with the chief inspector of homicide, Citta di Roma, and a photographer.

"You must vacuum the entire house, clean out the fingernails of the dead. Even dust, especially dust, can be important. Every sample you get will be checked with ours."

"What are we looking for?"

"Something imported. If it's there, you'll find it."

He looked at the worn cobblestones of the courtyard. Cigaret butts lay between the stones.

"We must have had thirty men here," the Roman detective shrugged.

"And thirty cars," Lupo frowned at the crisscross of tire tracks. "You examined this area before you parked?"

"No. Why?"

"Take a picture of every tire track here," Lupo told the photographer. "Every one to be blown up and transmitted by television to Naples. And do it now, before this place becomes a campground."

Lupo started back to his car. Another car came up the driveway and parked. A figure in a raincoat and carrying a pad approached.

"Dr. Lupo? I'm Phillips, International Wire Services,

Naples. We met at the Kinsdale press conference."

Lupo shook his head and kept walking.

"What are you doing here in Rome, Mr. Phillips?"

"The question is, what are you doing here in Rome? Is there a connection between this and the Kinsdale case?"

"I don't know," Lupo walked faster. "I don't know, Mr. Phillips, but I intend to find out."

The black of night was giving way. The Roman Colosseum rose, immense and pocked with decay, its stones blue in the predawn, above the scuttle of small, fast-moving cars. Edmonds' Ford screeched from a traffic light ahead of a swarm of Fiats.

"I have my hunches. One is that they're going to send yours truly to Naples to show our concern over the killings. I'll probably be told to deny everything."

A Fiat honked and jockeyed behind the Ford for passing room.

"We're all crazy, Frank, old boy. Just running around in little circles, getting narrower and narrower while we get picked off one by one."

"What's your other hunch?"

"The old cookie pusher's hunch?" Edmonds smiled. "All the U.S. agencies pass through me to track down everything from somebody's import license to their lost grandmother, you know what I mean? Well, a while back . . ."

Edmonds turned away from the Colosseum up the Via di San Giovanni. A Mercedes was coming the wrong way on the one-way street. Edmonds hit his power brakes hard. The Mercedes fishtailed to a stop a foot from the Ford's front bumper.

"Testa di cazzo!" Edmonds yelled out his window. *"Leviti!"*

"Ma va' a fan culo, stronzo Americano," the other driver yelled back.

"Stronzo yourself," Edmonds fumbled for his door handle. "I'll nail your . . ."

"Easy," Kinsdale grabbed Edmonds' arm. "It's not worth it."

Edmonds gave up on the door and sank back behind the wheel. He slammed the Ford into reverse and retreated about fifty feet.

"Nuts to that!" he said suddenly and jammed on the brakes. He slapped the shift into first. The Ford's rear wheels squealed and the big car shot forward, aimed directly at the Mercedes. At the last second, Edmonds' target jerked out of the way and half onto the sidewalk.

"Ha ha!" *Va-fan-gool* to you, too, fellah," Edmonds yelled as he raced past the Mercedes, "and a Merry Christmas!"

Edmonds slowed down to a steady sixty m.p.h., chuckling with self-satisfaction.

"You saw that car? According to Italian tax statistics, do you know how many people in this country earn over thirty thousand dollars? Thirty! There are Mercedes in the streets, yachts in the ports, you can't find a maid in Rome the demand is so high. But we keep bailing out these poor, honest Italians."

"That other hunch," Kinsdale persisted.

"Huh? Oh, yeah. I got this telex from the Bureau, the FBI, a routine indication that a certain U.S. citizen, Alexander Baldwin Taylor . . ." Kinsdale's head jerked from the road to Edmonds, "twice indicted for conspiring to incite a riot, former would-be big shot with the Students for a Democratic Society, is traveling to Europe. This is fairly routine."

"Routine?"

"Sure. We keep an eye out to see if he isn't taking

a crash course in bombmaking from some of the Red student groups here. O.K.

"Then I get another telex from the Narcs. One Alexander Baldwin Taylor, convicted on a minor drug charge in Massachusetts, has passed through Immigration at Fuimicino Airport. Keep your eyes open.

"Suddenly, the Treasury wires. Alexander Baldwin Taylor has written a check for five thousand dollars on the City Bank of New York here in Rome. Another cashed for five thousand on the Farmers in Boston. Et cetera, et cetera. Eventually, it all adds up to twenty-five thousand dollars worth of checks passed through a series of Rome and Naples banks in a matter of days. Check on this guy for possible irregularities.

"What am I supposed to do? Go to the Italian police? They're going to bust their butts to stop some American from spending his dough in their country?"

The Ford banked around the Piazza di San Giovanni. From beneath the front seat, something rolled against Kinsdale's feet. It had rolled against his feet earlier when Edmonds braked to avoid hitting the Mercedes. Kinsdale assumed then that it was a can of windshield cleaner or the like. Now he could tell it was bigger and heavier.

He reached down and pulled out a sawed-off Winchester pump shotgun. Edmonds, Kinsdale thought, was a man who took his paranoia seriously. But when was paranoia not paranoia?

Edmonds went right on talking while Kinsdale shoved the shotgun back under the seat.

"Anyway, I get a letter. A Mrs. Esther Baldwin from Boston. Her grandson, sweet Alexander, has emptied some trust funds to the tune of three hundred thousand dollars. Now they're an old Boston family, respected and so on, so they don't want to make a big deal. However, the friendly bank manager told her the naughty boy might be here so, as a taxpayer, she wonders if we couldn't call him in for a chat and talk him into going home. You like it?"

"It gets better?"

"Better yet, buddy. So I harass a tourist, like his grandma wants, using a friend I have at the desk of the Excelsior Hotel. Alexander Taylor, it seems, placed a lot of long-distance phone calls to a certain Hamshari in the Naples area. Hey, there's your car."

They'd left the Alfa on the Appia Nuova, close to the Autoroute for Naples. The Ford coasted to a stop behind the sports car.

"What about Hamshari?"

"Yassef Hamshari is a respected resident of Italy. Period. End of story. Taylor split from Rome and that's the last we know of him."

The sun was coming up fast. Kinsdale squinted as he got out of Edmonds' car and walked to his own. As he opened the door and slid in, Edmonds pulled alongside.

"Look," Edmonds was starting to sober up, "I probably am a load of . . . you know, this whole night was like a nightmare. I talk too much, I drink too much. Maybe I said something that'll help you, though, huh?"

"Could be."

"You'll let me know if something turns up, O.K."

"Don't worry," Kinsdale promised him, "You'll hear."

Kinsdale didn't drive straight back to Naples. He u-turned on the Appia Nuova and drove back across the center of Rome, past the hotels of the Piazza de la Republica to the fashionable Via Bissolati. Bissolati was a tourist thoroughfare of brassy clothes stores and sleek airline offices. He parked across from the Pan Am office and checked his watch; the time was 8:56.

He took his .45 from his belt and slid it into the Alfa's glove compartment. From the glove compartment, he removed a cordless electric shaver and began running it over his face.

Across the street, a young woman in a powder-blue hostess uniform arrived at the closed Pan Am office and unlocked the door. Kinsdale shaved faster.

He checked himself in the mirror. No more stubble, but the lines of his face were drawn and lean, a subtle transformation that had nothing to do with fatigue. Physically, he was paring down, he way a hunter did on a long stalk.

Inside the Pan Am office, Ground Hostess Sandra Pallavicini had just turned on the light switches when a big man in sunglasses entered carrying a briefcase. She could see he was American and greeted him in English.

"Good morning, sir. I'm afraid we won't be open for business for another twenty minutes."

"Morning. I'm Dave Edmondson," Kinsdale said, "from P.D.U. Services."

"Yes?" She didn't understand.

"I'm with the computer company," he smiled to put her at ease. "We've installed a new up-to-date logic circuit in London, and I'm putting all our agency terminals on the hookup." She still looked quizzical. "I'm supposed to do some work."

"Oh, sorry, Mr. Edmonson. I thought you were a customer. Really, the head office never tells us anything."

"May I?" he gestured to the computer terminal behind the desk.

"Please."

He sat himself purposefully at the terminal. The girl started flipping through the morning's collection of E.T.A.s, but he could feel her alert eye on his back.

"I hope, Mr. Edmonson, that you're not going to be long. We have a busy day ahead and it would be a big confusion."

"Don't worry, I'm in a hurry, too." He switched the terminal on, then punched DISPLAY, INPUT and OUTPUT. "But, Miss, I'll need at least two outside telephone lines."

She brought an extra phone to the terminal.

"Just push this button and dial nine."

"Thank you."

As she walked away, he dialed nine and five more digits.

"Combined Forces Europe," answered.

"Program Three."

While switching circuitry emitted its beeps, he studied the terminal. It was of European manufacture.

"Program Three," Mike McAllister answered sleepily.

"Good morning."

"Yes, John," alertness entered Mike's voice.

"Are you familiar with ITC computer model 7203?"

"Yes."

"Where can I link up to?"

"There should be an output jack on the right of the console."

Kinsdale looked on the side of the terminal and found the dimple of a jack. He opened his briefcase, took out two thirty-six-inch wires and plugged them, male to female, into the jack. With a screwdriver from the briefcase, he unscrewed the base of the phone and connected the two loose ends of the wires. He wet two fingers, touched the connections and jerked his hand back from the shock.

"O.K., I think I'm hooked up," he told Mike. "Try me."

The display of the airline terminal went blank.

"HELLO THERE" appeared on the screen.

"Fine," Kinsdale spoke into the phone. "What did you find out?"

"EDMONDS INFO CONFIRMED BUT NO APPARENT RATIONALE—STOP—HAVE TERRORIST DATA ASKED FOR—STOP—NO SHORTER THAN LAUNDRY LIST OF THE FREE WORLD"

"Maybe we can shorten it," Kinsdale said. "Stand by."

He unscrewed the base of the other phone and attached two more wires from that to the console. He dialed the second phone and an Italian voice replied.

"Internazionale."

"Do you speak English?"

"Yes, sir."

"I'd like to call the United States."

"What city?"

"Boston."

"You can dial direct. Do you know your area code?"

"Yes, thank you."

Kinsdale pressed the plunger and dialed again.

"A.T.S. Computer," came the answer from the other side of the Atlantic.

"This is A.T.S. Europe, Code 31783," Kinsdale said. "I want a positive feed link on the 903. Confirm."

"Number 31783, we accept that. I will give you a line now." Click.

Kinsdale cleared the terminal display and picked up the first phone, tucking it under his neck. He began typing.

"Mike, do you read this name on your screen? Yassef Hamshari. It's Arabic. I want to see if it turns up anywhere that Alexander Taylor has been. Interrogate Immigration. See if there's any record of this man in America."

A line of travelers waited outside the airline office. Sandra Pallavicini caught Kinsdale's eye.

"Coffee?" she asked amiably. The American looked very tired.

"Please, with milk."

"It'll be hot in a minute."

Primly organized, she pressed a button at her desk and the office doors slid open. The first customer entered, waving a dog-eared ticket. A durable smile spread on the hostess's lips.

"What's happening, Mike," Kinsdale asked on the phone.

"CROSS REFERENCES TO EDUCATION, IMMIGRATION, TREASURY — STOP — SHALL I FOLLOW?"

"Anywhere it goes. I want a link."

At that moment, a furious Dr. Enrico Lupo was leaving the office of the ambassador of the United States. In his hand was a rolled up morning edition of *Tempo,* the newspaper's headline screaming about the massacre at EUR. A charge d'affaires trotted after Lupo.

"Doctor, your attitude . . ."

"Where's Morrisey, your Signor Morrisey of the CIA?" Lupo wheeled.

"We . . . we don't have an office of the CIA here."

"Where?"

"You might try the Political Office. First floor," the charge stammered, "room . . ."

Morrisey didn't "happen" to be in the Political Office. He was the political officer. He was smoking his first cigar of the day and hanging up the phone when Lupo pushed the office door open.

"Heard you were on the . . ."

"When were you going to tell me we were working with a political time bomb?" Lupo brushed aside the agent's hand.

"Ah," Morrisey paused innocently, "you weren't informed?"

"Possibly the ambassador considered me a security risk. I've just *been* informed. And what about our 'frank' exchange of information, you talked about. I'd like a transcript of your Fonseca interrogation, but I would have liked it more yesterday."

"What?"

"Your interrogations in Naples. You have a man there now."

"No. Sometimes, the embassy sends Edmonds down, but . . ." Morrisey squashed his cigar out. "What about this interrogation?"

"Oh," Lupo slapped the newspaper against his leg, "we'll try to keep you informed."

The chief inspector turned and walked out.

Information was coming quickly into the airline computer from Program Three.

"FBI REPORTS TAYLOR AN SDS DROP-OUT; CONSIDERED THEM TOO INEFFECTIVE . . . DEAN'S LIST AT BERKELEY; MAJOR: INTER-

NATIONAL AFFAIRS . . . ALTOGETHER, FLY-
WEIGHT ACTIVIST WITH A HEAVY WAL-
LET. . . .

"YASSEF HAMSHARI . . . PALESTINIAN
PROFESSOR . . . AT BERKELEY TAUGHT PO-
LITICAL SCIENCE AND MIDEASTERN STUD-
IES; LIKELY HE HAD TAYLOR AS A STU-
DENT. . . .

"IMMIGRATION RECORDS HAMSHARI AS
ACTIVIST IN MIDEAST POLITICS IN 1940'S . . .
CONSIDERED OF MODERATE VIEWS SINCE
. . . CURRENTLY ON SABBATICAL FROM UCLA
. . . STILL????"

The airline hostess approached with a paper cup of
coffee from the other side of the computer counter. She
placed the cup on top of the display, which she couldn't
see.

"It's working all right, Mr. Edmonson?"

"You'd be amazed. Thanks," Kinsdale picked up the
cup. He sipped with pleasure for her benefit and she
returned to Pan Am's globetrotters. He picked up the
phone again.

"Mike, Taylor was involved in radical groups. If
this Hamshari character is still active we have the
start of an Italian cell. Can you link the two of them
with Al Fatah or any of the underground guerrilla
movements in Italy? Any link at all?"

"DATA COMING IN FROM IMMIGRATION . . .

"SON OF YASSEF HAMSHARI, PAUL KAMAL
HAMSHARI, TWENTY-SIX, NATURALIZED
AMERICAN LIKE FATHER AND SISTER,
MARINA . . . PAUL HAMSHARI A HEAVY-
WEIGHT RADICAL ORGANIZER AT BERKELEY
. . . CONFIRM FROM FBI

"LEFT USA FOR BELGIUM FOUR MONTHS AGO ... LAST SEEN IN BRUSSELS TWO MONTHS AGO, WHEN QUESTIONED ABOUT RAID ON NATO ARMORY ... RELEASED FOR LACK OF EVIDENCE ... NO KNOWN ADDRESS. ..."

"An address for any of the Hamsharis?" Kinsdale asked.

"ONLY FOR MARINA HAMSHARI ... A BOUTIQUE CALLED 'CIRCO MAGICO' ON CAPRI. ..."

George Edmonds ushered the brusque Italian detective into his office. Probably some inane questions about any "enemies" poor Bill Simpson could have had, Edmonds assumed. He perched on the edge of his desk, expecting the Italian to sit and get comfortable.

"Shall we get right to it, Mr. Edmonds?" Lupo remained standing.

"Gladly," Edmonds smiled, "though you're the first public official this year not to have coffee first."

Lupo was not amused.

"I have met with a certain Mr. Fonseca."

"Oh?" Edmonds shrugged.

"You should know him. I believe you met him."

"Is that so?" What the hell did this have to do with Bill Simpson, Edmonds wondered.

"Mr. Edmonds," Lupo grew angry, "you think Americans and Italians have to be at odds in this investigation? Is that your point?"

"Inspector, Dr. Lupo, I'm sorry. I don't understand you."

"You had certain information that led you to suspect Mr. Fonseca. You know, the one with red hair."

"I what? Now, wait a minute. I don't like your insinuations. I don't even know what you're talking about. What investigation?"

"I'm talking," Lupo enunciated, "about the Kinsdale and Simpson massacres. You did not go to Naples to interview Fonseca?"

"I've, I've been to Naples many times," Edmonds admitted, "but I haven't been there for a month."

"But, I've learned that you are the only man in this embassy besides the CIA with a police pass from our ministry."

"Which I got last night so I could go to the Simpson house. Here!" Edmonds went around his desk and yanked open a drawer. He took a green plastic card out and slapped on his desk top. "Take it. Look at the date. Then I have a few million things I want to tell you about the efficiency of Italian police, Dr. Lupo."

The card was one day old. Lupo dropped it back on the desk.

Edmonds poured one glassful of scotch at his office credenza and stared out of his window while he tried for self-control. First Simpson, then a night without sleep, now this clown.

"Dr. Lupo," he said softly. He turned away from the window and set the scotch down without a sip. "Wait a minute . . . wait a minute . . . an American who talked to me last night at the Simpson place had a pass. He said he was with CID. I checked him out this morning and neither CID nor the CIA had ever heard of him."

"What was his name, what did he look like?"

"Frank Evans, he said. Wore sunglasses of all things. Was . . ."

"Wait," Lupo interrupted. "Let me tell you. Tall, well-built, hair prematurely white."

"Yes," Edmonds gaped.

"And, what did you tell him last night?"

Edmonds massaged his face. His memory was clouded by a hangover, but he could recall saying a lot more than a foreign service officer should if he wanted to ever reach his pension.

"Nothing, nothing much."

"Sure?"

"Positive." He watched Lupo go toward the door. "But you described this guy. You know him."

"Learning to know him," Lupo said slowly, as if more to himself than anyone else.

VII

Riding high above the water, the Aliscafi hydrofoil from Naples took only twenty minutes to reach the subtropical paradise called the Isle of Capri. Separated by the Bay of Naples from all the pollution, poverty and anarchy of the rest of Italy, the four-mile-long island was a fantastic and colorful limestone yacht on which the rich could ride out financial and social turbulence. Juniper, acanthus and myrtle flowed down the walls of Monte Solaro like a vertical garden of Eden. Painters and patrons walked down the steps of Capri at an indolent pace, for here the sky was always as clear as the azure sea, it was never too hot or too cold and crime was something read about in day-old newspapers.

Seeking a glimpse at such a paradise, the hydrofoil's passengers disembarked at Marina Grande. Kinsdale was among them, in search of something else.

On the pier, he questioned a fisherman, who pointed to a diminutive piazza of sidewalk cafés and tourist-oriented gift shops. The cafés all had outdoor tables shielded from the sun by parasols bearing the brand name "Cinzano." The gift shop windows were decorated with fishing nets and seashells and credit card emblems. The farthest shop had a driftwood sign carved with the title "Circo Magico."

"Could anything be cuter?" A woman in a straw hat pointed at the straw hat worn by a carriage horse. "Let's ride up in that one."

Foursomes of women rushed to the carriages which would cart them up to the town of Capri. Less extravagant tourists headed for buses or the funicular, all but Kinsdale, who had found what he wanted and was patting his gun as he walked.

The "Circo Magico" sold light silk and cotton dresses, bikinis and leather handbags. A blonde saleswoman was at the desk reading a copy of *Elle*.

"Can I help you?"

"Are you Marina Hamshari?"

"No. Back there," she gestured to the rear of the shop and went back to glossy pages inhabited by undernourished models.

Behind a shop divider of tinsel seaweed, Kinsdale found an attractive, dark-haired girl serving a middle-aged German couple. The frau stood in a bikini in front of a mirror looking at a reflection as inviting as bandaged dough. While the husband issued encouragement in German, Marina Hamshari turned with a smile at Kinsdale's step. Not just attractive, Kinsdale realized. The girl was beautiful. Wide-apart black eyes, a delicate nose and an olive complexion.

"Marina Hamshari?"

"That's me. Can I help you."

The woman in the bikini twisted to see her ample rear in the mirror.

"I'm with the American consulate," Kinsdale said in a low voice. "I need some information about your brother, Paul."

"Yes . . ." the girl tensed.

"He's been collecting American Express cards."

"I see," Marina nodded, with what Kinsdale took as relief.

The German woman tapped Marina's arm.

"Is der von das ist bigger here und ambision smaller here?"

"Umm, no, I'm sorry," the girl answered, distracted. "That's the end of the line."

"Das ist a pity."

The German couple conferred and made their way into a dressing room.

"I can't talk now, I'm working," Marina said quickly." I have lunch in fifteen minutes. We can discuss what you want then, in private. Please."

He'd expected as much, and he had the right meeting place in mind.

"Very well. I'll be waiting at the pier."

Marina waited until Kinsdale was out of the door of the "Circo Magico" before she went to the phone.

Kinsdale was busy at the pier, where a motor launch with rows of seats was tethered. Its captain sat on a piling eating fried squid.

Visits to the Grotta Azura, he answered Kinsdale's question, cost 300 lira round trip. He looked at the 300 lira Kinsdale laid down beside the squid. But no trips would be going until at least twelve passengers were aboard. Kinsdale counted out another 3,300 lira. But it was lunchtime, the captain protested.

"You're not going," Kinsdale added 10,000 more lira to the pile.

* * *

Marina Hamshari was punctual. With her was a gaunt man with gray hair and eyes that scanned John Kinsdale like a hawk's.

"My father, Yassef Hamshari," she said nervously. "This is . . . I'm sorry, I missed your name."

"Edmonds. George Edmonds," Kinsdale said. Neither man offered to shake hands.

"You said something about credit cards," Yassef Hamshari said.

Kinsdale looked around the port. Light, dappled by the water, reflected a sun so bright he almost had to squint in spite of his sunglasses.

"It's terrible," he said conversationally, "but in all my years with the consulate I never got to Capri. You sure are lucky to live in a place like this. Just gorgeous. I hope you don't mind, but I thought since I was here I could mix business with pleasure and take a little boat ride."

"Mr. Edmonds . . ." Hamshari began.

"That should be private enough for our talk, too."

Before the father and daughter could react, Kinsdale picked up Marina and placed her in the launch.

"Mr. Hamshari," he waved for the old man to take his turn. "I bet you can make it by yourself."

Kinsdale got behind the wheel and pushed the ignition button. Two Evinrude inboards kicked to life. He cast off.

As the launch headed west through the port, Kinsdale kept an eye open for any other boats hurriedly leaving the docks. "Private" was a word open to definition. It could mean a room locked and bolted, where a conversation with the girl could end with a bullet from an air vent. Or it could mean the open sea, with hostages and no surprises. His hostages this time, not theirs.

"Where are we going!" Marina tried to shout over the sound of the engines. Her father pulled her back in her seat.

"We'll know when we get there," Hamshari told her. "Whatever Allah wills." But his eyes bored into Kinsdale with steady alertness.

The launch traversed two miles of Capri's northern coast before Kinsdale headed in to a break in the limestone cliffs. Engines in neutral, he coasted by jagged, outlying rocks. The island's limestone was worn and contorted by millennia of waves. Caves appeared, some darting out of sight, others bright from sun pouring down through sinkholes in the cliffs.

At the largest cave was a small dock of deserted boats and an empty ticket booth. Across the mouth of the cave was a chain with the sign "Grotta Azzura—The Blue Grotto." A paper taped to the window of the booth read, *"Chiuso."*

"That's Italy," Kinsdale lifted a hand. "In lunchtime, everything closes."

He inched the boat forward. The chain hit its windshield and, growing taut, rattled up. The Hamsharis ducked as the chain, reverberating, snapped over the top of the windshield. The launch slipped into the grotto.

No direct sunlight entered the cave. Instead, light refracted deep in the water rose up from its surface. Underwater rocks, twisted into grotesque shapes by wave action, took on a silver glow. The vaulting walls of the grotto, reaching 100 feet at its roof, were suffused by a surreal, blue energy.

With its motor off, the launch drifted toward the center of the cave.

"You have been here before," Hamshari said.

Sound waves, trapped as completely as light, rebounded from water to ceiling and from one dank, blue wall to another.

Been here before, here before, before.

"Yes," Kinsdale turned to face the Hamsharis. With my family, not with you, he nearly added.

"You didn't come about any credit cards," Hamshari said.

"No."

Hamshari closed his eyes for a moment.

"You would like to arrest my son," he said.

"No. I've only come to talk to him. Do you know where he is, Mr. Hamshari."

"I haven't seen my son for almost two months. And, that's all I or my daughter have to say."

Kinsdale brought out the .45 from his belt and laid it on his lap.

"I almost expected that, Mr. Edmonds," Hamshari sighed.

"Don't," Marina Hamshari started begging. "He doesn't know anything. Don't shoot."

"But he does," Kinsdale said softly. "He knows where Kamal is. Where?"

"I am so old," Hamshari focused on the automatic, "I can accept death. But I don't believe you would harm my daughter. I would not harm yours."

"Your son would!" Kinsdale lifted the gun level with Hamshari's narrow chest. "I want him. Where is he?"

"Please, Mr. Edmonds," the girl cried.

"Where, damn you?"

Some old steel came into Hamshari's eyes.

"I will repeat, I don't know. Now, if you wish, you may kill me."

Kinsdale fired. The wooden bench between Yassef

Hamshari and his daughter split open into a jagged crown of raw splinters. Around and throughout the grotto the same terrible clap boomed like the disorderly report of a firing squad.

Marina Hamshari fell on her knees, clutching her father and sobbing.

"My father is innocent! He did nothing!"

A second round was in the .45's breech.

"No one is innocent," Kinsdale whispered.

"It's all right, all right," Hamshari caressed his daughter's hair. He looked up. "You enjoy terrorizing us."

"Tell him, Daddy. He's mad."

"Right. I am mad," Kinsdale agreed.

"Daddy, please don't die . . ."

Hamshari lifted Marina back onto the bench. He held her tight as he talked.

"You see, unlike my son, my daughter still needs me. Kamal? His faith in humanity is less than mine. Moderation is not today's most passionate cause, and passionate young men believe that for change and justice there must first be total destruction. To be honest, I once believed that myself. Yes, the same dark vision of my son. Perhaps it was his inheritance from me. It was not the one I wished him to have, but you're right. I cannot claim complete innocence. My daughter can, though. As could yours, Mr. Kinsdale."

Kinsdale blinked as if he'd been slapped.

"I knew as soon as I saw you at the dock," Hamshari continued. "I saw the television report of the tragedy earlier. Now, your pallor, the red marks from the glasses. I am very sorry for you."

Kinsdale lifted off his glasses. For the first time, he was aware of the rawness around his nose and ears.

"I saw the hatred, too," Hamshari said, "the all-consuming hatred that turns to madness. I knew it long ago. What is truly unfortunate is that you are only learning to hate now. An appropriate place, this grotto, like an entrance to Hell from which there is never a return. Once you kill us."

The .45 hung slackly in Kinsdale's hand.

"I can sympathize with a man who has lost his family. I," Hamshari patted his daughter's shoulder, "have lost Kamal, just one son. But I have lost him. We do not talk and I do not know where he is. Now, if you still intend to kill us in spite of what I have told you, please go ahead."

Kinsdale sat bowed over the automatic for an endless minute. Then he slipped the .45 back into its holster. At a push of the button, the inboard engines came to life again.

VIII

Mike was in the War Room when Kinsdale returned.

"Sorry I'm late," Kinsdale set his briefcase on his console. "How's it going?"

"Fine," Mike watched his friend from the corner of his eye. "We've got a program going for a limited nuclear scenario in Yugoslavia. If you want to begin the prime programming, we can start any time."

"No," Kinsdale looked up sharply from his opened briefcase. "I want a complete profile on Kamal Hamshari. I'm convinced that . . ."

"I know, John. But the wolves are at the door. General Fuller wants this one and I can't stall him forever."

"What do you mean?"

"I mean that your special programs and linkups are beginning to absorb a lot of our computer time."

"Simulate a breakdown," Kinsdale sorted notes from his briefcase.

"John, I agreed to help you, but . . ."

Mike's eyes avoided Kinsdale's.

"What's changed your mind?"

"Well," Mike answered reluctantly, "you're not telling me everything."

"No?"

"No. For instance, I see we're feeding and computing data from the Delaware Bay Institute. Who or what are they?"

Kinsdale put his hands in his pockets and walked slowly to the center of the War Room. The world display was on satellite track. Hundreds of ruby and blue blips moved over the screen. The Mediterranean display was on underwater surveillance, pinpointing red and blue submarines located by sensors moored to the ocean floor.

"What I am doing is what I always, what we always do, Mike. Formulating a game plan." Even to himself, Kinsdale's voice sounded tinny and mechanical. "The prime requisite is the absorption of all available data on the enemy."

"The Delaware Bay?"

"The Delaware Bay is an institute that evaluates human behavior. I feed them what I know about my targets and they give me a psychiatric profile."

"For what?"

"To act. When I have the highest probability possible, when I am absolutely certain that these are the people . . . when there is no reasonable doubt . . ."

"Then you give all this information to the police?" Mike asked. "They arrest these ciphers that Program Three has packaged up so neatly?"

"Right!"

"Wrong! I've just been looking at another personality profile," Mike held up a printout, "and I didn't have to go to Delaware Bay for it. Janice gave it to me. I'm reading, 'Kinsdale, John, in confrontation with the targets, based on the assumptions posed in profiles recorded, will attempt to terminate targets. Probability of success—68 percent.' "

The game screen was blank. Kinsdale stood in front of it, a motionless silhouette.

"Are you really going to try to kill them, John? Do you want to be just like them?"

If there had been a moment when Kinsdale doubted, when he faltered—as with Yassef Hamshari—that moment was erased. Because now he had the single, most important data of all: the statistical edge. And it was his.

The phone on his desk rang. It kept ringing until Mike lifted the receiver.

"It's for you, John. A Dr. Lupo is coming through the gate."

Lupo at Program Three. Kinsdale snapped out of his reverie.

"Tell him I'll meet him in my office."

Mike relayed the message.

"Oh, by the way," Mike said as he hung up. "A girl called from the employment agency today. She insisted on speaking with you, but I put her off. She may call back."

"From the employment agency? Yeah, I rememeber. Ann . . . was advertising for help in the . . ."

Kinsdale put a fist to his mouth. He was on the phone to Ann and she said the doorbell rang, probably the girl. . . . He snatched a copy of the *Daily American* from Mike's desk and turned to the classified section. His home phone number was still listed.

"Mike, do you remember the Simpson telephone number? Was it 868-551?" Kinsdale's finger rested on another listing.

"That sounds right. Why?"

If a killer wanted to find an American family to wipe out, how would he find the right one? How would he get through the door? Kinsdale had the answer but he no longer had help. He couldn't trust Mike anymore.

"You better get up to sub-level Two to see this Lupo," Mike advised.

"Sure," Kinsdale put the newspaper under his arm. "See you."

Kinsdale took the elevator. As soon as the doors had closed and the car began moving, he hit the Stop button. It halted, suspended between floors. Kinsdale lifted the car's emergency phone.

"No trouble," he told the guard who answered, "but this is an emergency call and I need an outside line. . . . This is John Kinsdale and I have total clearance so you get me that line now!"

Lupo would be making the long walk from the gate. Kinsdale's outside line came and, frantically, he started down the list of ads for English-speaking domestic help and au pair girls.

The inspector would be escorted and the marines at the entrance to Program Three would hold him up until a visitor's pass was made out in his name. A minute, a minute and a half at the most.

". . . No one called? No, that's perfectly all right. Thank you, Mrs. Johnson," Kinsdale hung up, lifted the phone and immediately dialed again. Every two days, the ultimatum had said; this was the sceond day since the Simpson deaths.

"Mrs. Gerardi? Your number is 358-924, an Amalfi exchange, right?" Kinsdale asked. "I'm with the *Daily American*. You placed an ad in our paper a few days ago, and I'm checking to see what results we're getting with our advertising. Have you had any calls? . . . You

did? . . . She called this morning for when? . . . Ten
o'clock, and your address is where? . . . 1324 Belve-
dere, Amalfi. Yes, I can see it on our file. Thank you,
Mrs. Gerardi, sorry to have troubled you. Goodbye."

Shaking, he put the phone back in its cradle and
released the Stop button.

He was as composed as a machine when the chief
inspector entered his office forty seconds later.

"Signor Kinsdale, it's time we had another talk."

"Good," Kinsdale shut the door and led Lupo to a
chair. "Sit down. Tell me how the investigation is
getting along."

"A better question," Lupo sat, "is how your investigation is progressing. Signor, you stole a pass from
my office. Don't interrupt, please. You stole a pass,
which I never would have suspected. You interrogated
a Mr. Fonseca, after which I had, entertained let's say,
some doubts about you. Then you were at the Simpson
house and spoke to a Mr. Edmonds."

"Gee," Kinsdale threw up his hands, "I wish I knew
what the hell you were talking about."

"What interested me was how you were at each
place, spoke to all these people before I did. A curious
situation, even a little embarrassing for me. A mere
computer programmer first with every clue, first at the
scene of each crime? I understand now that you are
no mere programmer, are you? You are, in fact, chief
war programmer. Even a genius in your trade."

"I'm just another civil servant on overseas duty."

"I know the cover story. How many Americans in
Italy have ones like it," Lupo frowned. "A programmer
of death. Didn't what happened to your family, the real
deaths of your wife and children, teach you the difference between the statistics of a computer and human

lives? I'm trying to tell you this is no game, Signor Kinsdale! And this is my job, not yours in spite of all the gadgetry you might have at your disposal."

"Doctor Lupo, if that's all you have to tell me, I'm a busy man."

"That's not all." From his jacket pocket, Lupo took a dark rag. "A disraught man following an investigation would be one thing. I had to make sure you were not something else, so I took the liberty of revisiting your house. In the bedroom, I found what was left of a television set and this cloth, which is permeated with gun oil. I want the gun, Signor Kinsdale, and I want you out of my way."

"What do you mean?"

"Protective custody, for your own good until this investigation is concluded."

Kinsdale felt the room closing in. Custody? House arrest now that he finally knew where they would strike next?

"Shall we go?" Lupo stood.

"Wait. Look, this is all top security work. Maybe I have been going off half-cocked, but if I walk out with you it's going to look like a straight-out arrest, like I was a suspect. I'd lose my security clearance and I wouldn't get work again in years. You go. Give me a minute and I'll follow. It's a pretty damn small favor, Doctor. I'll be right out."

Lupo hesitated.

"Right after you," Kinsdale repeated.

"Very well. But," Lupo put out his hand, "the keys to your car, please."

Kinsdale handed them over.

"My men and I will be waiting in our car outside the gate," Lupo said.

Four minutes later, an increasingly impatient Lupo rolled down the rear window of a black police sedan.

"Some one is coming out now, Doctor," his driver said.

Lupo focused field glasses on the entrance of Program Three. It was Kinsdale, waving goodbye to the marine guards. Kinsdale moved at a casual pace into the parking lot. Lupo watched him stop by an Alfa Romeo.

"He won't get far with that," Lupo thought of the car keys.

Kinsdale reached into the sports car. Lupo could see him picking something up and slipping it into the belt.

"Good, he's bringing the gun with him. Wait, what is he up to now?"

A jeep cruised in front of the bunkerlike building. Kinsdale hopped in the back.

"Start the car," Lupo slapped the driver on the back.

The jeep headed from Program Three on an interior road. On the road outside the gate, the police car rode parallel with the jeep. Lupo glanced up at passing signs.

"Commissary — Veterans' Affairs — Community Room — American Personnel, Dependents and Employees Only"

"We can go in there. He can't get away," the policeman in back with Lupo said. "My brother works there, comes and goes all the time."

Lupo had followed the trail of the war gamer across half of Italy; he wasn't so sure the American could be trapped anywhere.

They lost sight of the jeep in a parking lot crammed with station wagons, families, shopping carts and delivery trucks. The police car swung into the lot and jammed its brakes. Lupo jumped out, scanning the complex of buildings with his glasses. He spotted the jeep; there was no Kinsdale in the back.

"We'll just tell the Americans they'd better find him," the driver handed Lupo the mike of the car radio.

A bus was coming out of the lot. It was a vehicle clearly meant for employees only. Dirty, rattling without a muffler, it was loaded to twice its legal occupancy. Employees, seeing the police, stuck out their hands with the gesture of the evil eye. As the bus passed, Lupo stepped into the middle of the road.

More passengers were hanging onto the poles of the bus's open doors. One of the hanging riders was Kinsdale.

Kinsdale watched the police car u-turn and Lupo jump in. A net bag of tomatoes and frozen chicken bounced into his face as the bus picked up speed through a red light. A Coca-Cola truck swung into the commissary road, blocking the police car.

The bus turned onto the Via del Duomo, headed for the center of Naples. Eighty yards back, the police car was gaining. Its siren cut in. The bus passengers looked back, laughing, while the driver held his accelerator flat down to the floor.

Two trucks full of melons and squash came out of a side street in front of the police car. Lupo's sedan danced from side to side trying to pass. He was going to get away, Kinsdale thought, until he felt the bus's brakes shrieking. He swung precariously from the pole. The police car ducked between the trucks. Lupo was only forty yards behind now, but a stream of nuns on bicycles wheeled into his path. The police car swerved sideways.

Kinsdale looked ahead. The bus was nearly at the Piazza Amore roundabout but nearly wasn't enough.

The whole traffic circle was a tangle of stalled and honking cars. He looked back. The police car was overtaking the bus on the driver's side. At once, the bus shuddered to a halt.

Kinsdale jumped to the street. More cars were piling into the roundabout. Three ranks of cars were between him and the sidewalk. He squirmed around a Lancia.

"Polizia!" Lupo and two of his men appeared at the front of the bus.

Kinsdale ducked behind the Lancia, inching his way forward.

"Kinsdale! Stop!"

Lupo reached for Kinsdale, one car width away. Kinsdale climbed away from the grasping hand and onto the hood of a Mercedes limousine. From the Mercedes, he ran, like a circus acrobat, across the hoods of three more cars.

"This way," Lupo shouted to his men.

The inspector squeezed between car fenders. In the middle of the traffic snarl, five husky Neapolitans were lifting a Fiat 500 complete with its driver off the street and onto the sidewalk. Beyond them, he saw Kinsdale running between pedestrians.

On the Via Corso, an outdoor food market had opened to catch the business of office workers. Kinsdale dodged around the vendors and buyers. A cardboard stall of oranges spilled over the sidewalk. Shouts and curses followed Kinsdale. Lupo, following, provided a better target for their fury. The orange vendor, a beefy grandmother, whipped her change purse into the police inspector's forehead, staggering him.

Kinsdale spun into a narrow sidestreet. Clotheslines zigzagged overhead, shirts, dresses, underwear almost blocking out the sun. His legs moved woodenly, the result of days without sleep. Stray cats, refuse and loose cobblestones tried to trip him. He looked over his shoulder. Lupo had entered the street and, as Kinsdale watched, the police car pulled up beside the inspector. Lupo got into the car, which accelerated after Kinsdale. The car's siren caromed through the street.

Kinsdale was almost at the next corner when a young man in a T-shirt moved to block him off.

"Ladro!"

The man swung. Running full tilt, Kinsdale ducked under the punch and rammed his shoulder into the man's chest. The would-be hero shot into a pile of garbage cans and bounced back into the street, bringing the cans with him.

"Stronzo!" Lupo's driver shouted.

The police sedan screamed sideways up onto the high sidewalk and smashed its headlights against a stoop. Two detectives jumped out to drag the man and kick the cans out of the street while the driver put the car in reverse. With all the police back in, the car burned rubber around the corner.

The next street was a dead end, but Kinsdale had disappeared.

Lupo got out.

"Go to the end of the street," he ordered the driver.

The buildings were all three-story tenements. There were probably a thousand apartments in all. Lupo didn't relish a door-to-door search for a desperate man with a gun. He rubbed the welt on his forehead.

At the end of the street, the sedan screeched to a stop and the men piled out. Lupo motioned detectives to move slowly back towards him and for the driver to stay where he was. The driver answered with a finger pointing above Lupo's head.

Lupo looked up. Three stories up, Kinsdale was running along the edge of a roof.

The inspector ran into the building.

Kinsdale moved from the streetside of the roof to the rear, where he looked down on a family partaking of coffee and cake on their second-story patio. The paterfamilias was stretched out at his ease on a beach chair, his espresso cup balanced on his stomach.

Kinsdale dropped, landing on all fours and rolling expertly into a potted lemon tree.

"*Scusa, scusa,*" he apologized to the little girl gawking at him. Her mother clamped her hand over a mouthful of *panettone*. The father gaped at the scalding coffee spreading over his shirt.

There was an iron fire escape leading from the patio to an alley.

"Kinsdale!"

Lupo, exhausted, was on the upper roof. Kinsdale saluted him and went down the fire escape, four steps at a time.

In the alleyway, a delivery boy put his Vespa scooter on its stand and carried a box of groceries to the rear of a house. At the sound of the scooter, he let the box fall and ran back into the alley to see a big man racing it through a pack of startled cats.

Groaning, Lupo ran to the front of the roof.

"He's on a scooter," he shouted down to the detectives. "Get in the car. He'll come out at the corner. Block him."

In reverse, the police sedan whined from the dead end, slowing just enough for the detectives to jump in. As the car reached the corner, Kinsdale came out of the alleyway. He steered around the battered grille of the Lancia, leapt the sidewalk, looped the car, dropped back on the street and accelerated away. Still in reverse, the car followed.

Shaking his head, the hero in the T-shirt had just

gotten to his feet when the Vespa clipped him and spun him into the street.

"No!" Lupo's driver saw the figure in the street again.

For a second time, he swerved onto the sidewalk. As he cut the engine, he listened to the tinkling of tail-lights.

The Amalfi coast, south of Naples geographically, far above it in tourist chic, was a romantic nighttime ride of postcard fishing villages and three-star hotels. The Gerardi home was actually a compound, two American-style ranch houses and a three-car garage set on a cliff overlooking the sea.

It was early; 9:40 by Kinsdale's watch. He coasted in on the scooter with the engine off to the kichen door. The sound of an Italian variety show came from an open window. He touched the kitchen door's bell button lightly.

"I'll get it," a woman's voice said. "It's probably Aldo."

The door opened to reveal a short woman in a pant-suit. At the sight of Kinsdale's disheveled appearance she started to shut the door, but he'd already insinuated his foot.

"Mrs. Gerardi?"

"Yes," she answered guardedly.

He entered and shut the door behind him. Pots and colanders, freshly washed and dried, hung from hooks. Along the cabinets was a supply of instant coffee. Nothing had happened; he was in time.

"Your family's at home?"

She didn't answer. Something was wrong, though Kinsdale couldn't understand what. Kinsdale stepped past her toward the sound of the television.

A thick, balding man in a sports shirt was fiddling with the reception of the living room TV. A teenage girl with bushy hair did homework at a table. In the corner, her younger brother read an Italian comic book. Until Kinsdale entered. Then they stared at the interloper with a common hostility and calm.

"Mr. Gerardi?"

"That's right," the heavy man went on tuning the television.

"I want to speak to you for a minute in private."

"Sure," Gerardi said coolly and looked at his wife. "Honey, will you ask Aldo if he's finished on that car yet? He should be out back."

Mrs. Gerardi left the living room.

"You a cop?" Gerardi asked in a loud voice.

"No," Kinsdale was surprised. "You recently placed an ad in the *Daily American* for a household helper, and . . ."

"And you're it?" Gerardi laughed.

The girl was squinting out the window. Kinsdale went to the window and followed her gaze. Mrs. Gerardi was in front of the garage talking to a muscular man who had just finished washing a black Chrysler Imperial. The car washer took a gun from his pocket, covered it with a buffing rag and started for the house ahead of Mrs. Gerardi.

Kinsdale turned, with his .45 trained on Gerardi.

"What's his name, Aldo? Call him in. Tell him nothing's wrong."

"What's your game?" Gerardi asked, as if mildly concerned. The kitchen door opened and shut.

"I said, talk to him," Kinsdale hissed.

Gerardi took a deep breath and glanced at his son

and daughter, frozen where they sat.

"O.K. . . . O.K. Hey, Aldo! Come on in. It's all right. It's a friend of the family."

Aldo and Mrs. Gerardi came into the room. One look at Kinsdale's gun, and Aldo knew he'd been had. He looked toward his boss for orders and Gerardi shrugged.

"Take the gun out of the cloth with two fingers and slide it to me across the floor," Kinsdale directed.

Carefully, Aldo did as he was told. Kinsdale picked up the gun, a Smith & Wesson .38, and stuck it in his back pocket.

"Good." Kinsdale gestured to the sofa with his .45. "Everyone sit down there."

Gerardi nodded. He and his family gathered, squeezing together on the sofa cushions, Aldo perched on a sofa arm. Kinsdale noticed that the henchman's hands were tattooed and scarred.

"I don't know who you are, FBI or Treasury or what, but you're in a lot of trouble," Gerardi shook his head. "Because here I'm just a respectable olive oil exporter and you can take your extradition papers and you know what you can do with them. If you're real intelligent, you'll take your popgun and your ass straight back to Washington and tell them it was no go, Lou Gerardi didn't have anything new to say."

Lou Gerardi? *That* Lou Gerardi? Kinsdale could remember newspaper stories from years ago in the States, articles about arrests, hung juries and a rapid flight from New York.

"I didn't come for any of that," Kinsdale tried to explain. "I want to help you. Someone is coming here to kill you. Not for anything you've done, simply because you're Americans."

"What are you doing with that gun, Mister?"

The telephone rang. Mrs. Gerardi was already agitated and every impulse in her body urged her to release her tension, to stop twisting the lapel of her pantsuit jacket and answer the phone. On the fourth ring, she stood and moved toward the telephone table.

"Sit down," Kinsdale told her.

As if deaf, she continued to the ringing phone.

"I said, sit down!"

As she reached for the receiver, he fired. Mrs. Gerardi screamed. The phone, shattered, leapt against a wall.

"You son of a bitch," Gerardi came off the sofa.

"Make your wife sit down," Kinsdale turned the .45 back on Gerardi.

The "oil exporter" glared at Kinsdale, then at his wife, who shook with sobbing.

"Alice . . . Alice, honey. Hey, baby, come on back here and sit down next to me. Come on." He took her hand and led her back to the sofa. "As for you," he told Kinsdale, "you've had it now. Either me, or my friends, or the friends of my friends are going to take care of you. You're dead, right now."

"Soon, maybe," Kinsdale looked at his watch; it was 9:52. "Not quite yet."

He went around the room, turning down the lamps and the volume of the television set, then returned to sit across from the Gerardi family, his .45 on his lap, and waited. A miniature pendulum clock sat on the mantel, measuring time with hypnotic swings.

At 10:08, the clock's ticking was eclipsed by the sound of a car engine. Keeping away from the light, Kinsdale glimpsed out the window.

"They're here," he said softly. "There is a group of

men out there who think you are defenseless, Gerardi. They murdered my wife and children. They have come to murder yours. Not because of what you do. Because you're American. We're in this together."

Footsteps came to the front door. The door's chimes rang. The Gerardis stared at Kinsdale.

"Hello. . . . Anybody home?" a girl's voice called through the door.

Kinsdale motioned Mrs. Gerardi from the sofa. She moved stiffly, biting her lips. Mascara had run under her eyes. Kinsdale flattened heimself against the wall beside the door. Mrs. Gerardi crossed herself and opened the door.

Pidgeon stood smiling at the threshold. Her long blonde hair was done in a ponytail and she carried a student's bookbag on one shoulder.

"Are you Mrs. Gerardi?" she chirped.

"Yes . . ." the older woman trembled, "I am. Can I . . . help you?"

Pidgeon looked in at the family waiting anxiously on the sofa. Mrs. Gerardi's face had turned white.

"Well," Pidgeon backed away from the door, "maybe . . . I'd better. . . ."

She broke and ran toward a dark van parked in the compound driveway.

Kinsdale swung through the door. Crouched, both hands on the .45's butt, he fired two rounds over the girl's head at the van. The van's rear door immediately opened and a hooded figure carrying an automatic rifle jumped out.

Kinsdale dropped to one knee and fired again. The rifle answered. A sweep of heavy-caliber fire blew out the window behind Kinsdale.

A second hooded figure emerged from the truck. Kinsdale heard the Gerardis' door slam shut behind him, cutting off his retreat. Glass, wood and plaster broke up outside and inside the house. Hit in the arm, Kinsdale slumped to the grass. He fired from a prone position. A third figure coming out of the truck grabbed a leg and pitched onto the driveway. Divots of lawn kicked in front of Kinsdale. A fourth and fifth figure emerged from the truck.

A shotgun blast from an upper window made the figures pause. Another shotgun boomed from a first-floor window.

The figures retreated, picking up their wounded and firing cover bursts.

Kinsdale ran for the van. The one he'd hit was still being pulled in, one boot dragging over the driveway. The flash of automatic fire came from the van, but wide and high of Kinsdale. They pulled in their casualty. Kinsdale dove for the rear door, clutching its handle. The flash arrester of a G-3 rifle hit his cheek. He let go. The G-3 erupted, ripping up asphalt as Kinsdale rolled to the side. The van's door shut and it gained speed out the compound's gate.

Kinsdale dragged himself to his feet. His left jacket arm was wet with blood. He could rotate the arm and bend his fingers. "Acceptable losses" in the parlance of the war games, but he'd have to apply a tourniquet. Maybe he could clean up in the Gerardi's bathroom. He walked, exhausted, back to the house.

All the house's windows on the first floor had been blown in. The center of the front door showed a ragged hole where 7.6-caliber rounds had torn their way into the living room. They had to believe him now.

"Get your ass outta here, Mister," Gerardi called from the second-floor window, "or I'll blow your friggin' ass off."

Holding his arm, Kinsdale turned from the house to

the motor scooter he'd left lying in the bushes. On the way, he found the bookbag.

"You heard what he said," Aldo and a shotgun appeared at the living room window. "Beat it!"

Kinsdale draped the bookbag over the scooter's handlebars. As he rode down the driveway, he could hear the volume of the television being turned up.

"These bio-profiles," Morrisey told the darkened room, "have been prepared with the cooperation of the United States Intelligence Board and the Federal Bureau of Investigation. This is covert A-11 information and classified top secret."

At the click of a Carousel slide projector, the color photo of a young, redhaired man appeared on a screen.

"Alexander Baldwin Taylor, twenty-eight, American citizen, passport number B-4256319, son of a prominent Boston banker, attended University of California at Berkeley. Dropout, former SDS radical. Subject had made several trips to Italy. Last entry nine days ago. Believed to be carrying about two hundred thousand dollars in hard currency. Check your fact sheets for complete details. Last and only contact, with the family of Yassef Hamshari, Capri.

"By the way," Morrisey added parenthetically, "if you find any of this confusing, Doctor Lupo, just say so and I'll elaborate."

"For the first time," Lupo answered from the dark, "I am not confused."

Taylor was replaced by a still of a sallow, haggard man.

"Yassef Hamshari, age sixty-five, naturalized American citizen, passport number C-1556280. Professor of political science, Mideastern studies, U.C. at Berkeley. Arrived in Italy on extended leave from university, July 10, 1974. Subject is a respected academic, although politically active in Palestine 1932 to 1958."

Click. On the screen was Yassef Hamshari and his daughter, both smiling.

"Marina Hamshari, twenty-two, naturalized American citizen, passport number C-1347721. Graduate of U.C. at Berkeley, political science major. Classmate and friend of Alexander Taylor. Unaffiliated politically."

Lupo glanced at the radiant dial of his watch. It was 11:15 P.M. Late, but after the Kinsdale incident the Americans were finally telling what they knew.

Click. Projected on the screen was a handsome youth with jet-black hair and thick eyebrows. A mole marked his cheek almost like a beauty spot. His mouth was marred by what seemed like a habitual sneer.

"Paul Kamal Hamshari, twenty-five, naturalized American citizen, passport number C-1455970. Graduate of U.C. at Berkeley, psychology major, Dean's list student. Supported many ultra-left causes, denounced his father's moderate political views. Polarized a variety of fringe campus organizations. Subject entered Italy ten months ago. Spot surveillance showed he made contact with known militants of different backgrounds, recruiting for what end was not known. And now, for our late addition."

Click. A petite girl in the uniform of a Cuban militia officer. Her blonde hair was piled up inside her fatigue cap and she leaned on a Kalishnikov automatic rifle.

"Dorothy Pidgeon, twenty-three, from Bloomington, Indiana. High school dropout. Arrests for drugs, prostitution and carrying a concealed weapon. At age eighteen, joined Cuban sugarcane cutting volunteers, stayed in Havana for agitprop and military training, although shipped back for low intelligence and instability. Moved with Weathermen until she joined Taylor and Hamshari at Berkeley, after those two had graduated. Last seen in Brussels."

"Where the G-3s were stolen," one of the other Americans spoke up.

"You got it. Lights?"

The room, actually a basement under the American Naples consulate renovated for radio communications, turned a bright, sickly green under fluorescent bulbs.

"That's it, Doctor, what we've just been able to patch together. Of course," Morrisey added, "this Kinsdale factor is damned embarrassing. How he got the leads first, I'll never know. He's no ordinary guy, though."

"I can testify to that," Lupo agreed. "But Taylor and Kamal Hamshari, you call 'radical' and 'ultra-left.' Remember, the Italian Communist party is the most successful political organization in this country. Do you mean Taylor and Hamshari are affiliated with them? Or with what other group?"

"I wish they were. Finding these fish would be a lot easier if they had a direct affiliation with another group. But they're floaters, wildcatters. Anyway, we're finally pulling in some more men on this case. Home base for the task force will be Rome."

"Kinsdale is in Naples," Lupo commented.

"Well, let's hope we know the big picture better than him," Morrisey was a little irritated. "Our psych section says Kamal is an educated and extremely dangerous man with delusions of being a political messiah. His m.o. shows a definite psychological imbalance, with a predilection for violence. He wants instant recognition from all other dissident groups. He knows how to hit America at its weakest point—our citizens abroad. He's got a veneer of ideology, a quarter-of-a-million-dollar bankroll and a team of veteran, trained assassins. If he and Kinsdale ever meet, Kinsdale will get eaten alive."

Lupo looked at the silent radio and teletype.

"Tonight was going to be the third massacre, wasn't it?" he said. "It's after midnight. The deadline is past. Nothing's happened."

"Yeah, well," Morrisey said, "we just haven't heard. We don't know where they are."

"You don't know where Kinsdale is, either."

As soon as they'd driven the van in, they slammed the garage doors shut. One figure, his thigh bandaged, was helped out. The leader, dressed as were the rest in black sweater and pants but marked by a natural air of command, knelt to examine four large bullet holes in the lower part of the van body. He was young, with a mane of dark hair and a mole on his left cheek.

"He almost got the tank. That's what he was aiming for."

Taylor, pale and sweating, jumped out of the driver's seat.

"Who the hell was that bastard, Kamal? And those goddamned shotguns?"

"You're asking *me* who they were, Alex?" Kamal rose.

The other stacked rifles and moved to the second floor of the garage. Taylor fumbled under Kamal's stare.

"What do you mean by that?"

"I mean we were set up. Somebody knew we were coming."

"What are you telling me, Kamal? That we have a security leak, or that you had a better plan?"

"Both." He laid the barrel of his rifle across Taylor's chest. "These are my people and I don't want casualties. From now on we work my way, no more of these chicken-shit raids. Every two days? Something was bound to go wrong. Now we do it right, a real slaughter that'll make the whole world pay attention to us."

Janice Lowe, already in her pajamas and bathrobe, was doing some late-night reading when her apartment doorbell rang. She looked at her watch in surprise. The bell rang again.

The apartment was a controlled shambles, as usual. No matter; if it was a rapist, he wouldn't notice, and if it was a friend, a friend wouldn't mind.

She opened the door. Leaning on the corridor wall was Kinsdale in shirtsleeves, one arm bandaged with what was left of his jacket, his good hand carrying a bookbag.

"John! Dear God, come in."

She shut the door behind him. Kinsdale walked stiffly to an easy chair and let himself collapse.

"Your arm, John. We've got to fix that."

"Just a flesh wound," he grinned weakly, "but I do not advise driving a motor scooter for two hours with a flesh wound."

"Can you use a drink?"

"Pretty much . . ."

She went to the kitchen. He could hear her wrestling with an ice tray.

"The police are looking all over for you," she called.

"I know."

He turned the bookbag upside down on Janice's coffee table. A small handgun, a powder compact, a slip of paper with the Gerardi's address written in a childish scrawl, a pack of Winstons and a book of matches fell out. No papers, nothing with a name. Printed on the face of the match book, though, was *Café Greco—Pozzuoli*.

Janice stood over him, holding out a whiskey on the rocks, her eyes on the Beretta on her table.

"Still not taking any unreasonable chances, I see."

"Thanks," he took the drink and took a long sip.

She sat down across from him.

A machine? General Fuller was wrong. Machines did very little bleeding. Machines did not fall asleep with a glass in their hands. Machines did not change from kindness to killing at the removal of love.

Janice took the glass from Kinsdale's hand and sipped.

"Janice . . . " Kinsdale opened his eyes.

"Yes?"

"Can I stay here for a while?"

"You know you can."

IX

Kinsdale awoke. Sunlight the color of white wine poured into the bedroom. Janice stirred beside him, her hair brushing his shoulder.

He'd gone to sleep in a chair, he was sure of that. When or how he'd been moved into bed, he didn't know at all. He sat up and looked at his arm. A neat gauze pad was taped over the triceps muscle.

And Janice's green eyes were open.

"I'm sorry," he began. "I don't remember . . ."

"You didn't get here on your own power, and you were a ton of deadweight, thank you," she smiled.

He became aware of the fact that he was undressed down to his shorts. He couldn't see any nightgown strap on Janice.

"Did anything . . . ?" he blushed.

"In your condition?" her smile became a laugh. "Nothing. Hungry, soldier?"

"Yeah."

She twisted and reached a hot plate with a coffee pot and sweet rolls. He saw that her back was bare.

Her skin was smooth and fair and warm from sleeping. There was no denying she was an attractive young woman.

"I usually read in bed while the coffee perks," she turned back to Kinsdale. Her leg touched his.

"Janice ... what's all this about?"

"Reentry, John. Reentry into the human race. Some love, contact," her hand slid under the sheet to his chest, "to remind you what it was. To tell you that someone does care what happens to you now. That you do have something to lose."

He put his finger on her lips. She stopped talking and he kissed her lips, feeling her body fold into his.

"Janice, you are the sweetest girl in the world. Thank you. Maybe, when this is over ..."

"Maybe you'll still be alive?"

"You'll be the first to know."

The sound of a small compressor motor filled the garage. In white overalls, dust mask and goggles, Kamal adjusted the nozzle of a spray gun. He'd already patched the bullet holes in the van with putty. As he pressed the gun's trigger, a cloud of olive drab started covering the truck's black paint.

"Kamal?"

Pidgeon had come down from the garage's living quarters. In only a man's shirt rumpled from sleep, she looked like a waif.

"Kamal?" she touched his shoulder.

He started, then recognized her and turned off the compressor.

"Go back to bed."

"I've been waiting for you," she said in a little girl's whine.

"I'm busy."

"Can't somebody else do this? Can't Alex? You're tired and it's so early."

Kamal inspected his painted-over repair job. No one would notice.

"Alex wants to sleep late. Alex always wants to sleep late," he murmured.

Pidgeon caressed the back of his neck.

"Kamal, please. . . ."

"Go to bed."

"Kamal, is everything all right?"

He knocked her hand away and looked up at her.

"Oh, everything is great, except for our near disaster," he answered sarcastically. "And our poor, little rich boy sleeps on. Well, it was my mistake to use him in the first place. Not any longer. Now we'll do what we should have done from the start."

She looked at the wet olive-drab paint on the van.

"What's that, Kamal?"

"What Ché always said: 'You must go to the heart of the monster.' " He nodded to himself and soothed by the thought he ran his gloved hand inside Pidgeon's shirt to her hip. "Go to bed. Rest. Very soon, we'll be there."

Janice led Kinsdale into the parking lot of her apartment building. Shaved, his shirt washed and ironed, his sunglasses glinting in the bright light, he looked like any office worker headed for a nine-to-five job. Janice stopped at an ancient, powder-blue Volkswagen.

"You know the shift?" she asked.

"Sure."

She opened the door and reached inside.

"You can adjust the seat with this lever."

"Thanks." He moved the seat all the way back and squeezed in behind the wheel. She dropped the car keys in his hand. "Thanks, again."

Janice pushed the door shut.

"Take care of Agatha," she said with a half-smile, "she's all I've got."

She waited for him to turn the ignition. Kinsdale paused for a second.

"Janice, I know the difference."

"What difference?"

"Between war games and . . . this. You lose the game, take fifteen million dead, a thousand aircraft, whole cities. You sit down, work a new equation, write out a new program for the computers. Erase your old tape and start the game again. But . . . some madmen come into your home and kill your wife and your kids? No new tape, no new game. That's it."

Kinsdale started the Volkswagen.

"That Italian inspector didn't think I knew the difference," he told Janice. "I know the difference."

Alexander Taylor, puffy-eyed with sleep, putting on his shirt and tucking its tails into his pants, came down to the garage. No one was here, either. Bastards hadn't even gotten him up. The van was gone as well. He wrinkled his nose at the smell of paint. What the hell was going on?

He scratched himself. He was hungry, too, and he didn't feel like cooking for himself. His watch said 11:14. Rifles, explosives, even the detonator was gone. Where were they?

The Café Greco, he answered himself. Probably lounging around there stuffing themselves on greasy pizza when they should have waited for him to tell

them what to do next. He was going to have to talk to
Kamal. Kamal was geting out of hand.

He fished a prescription envelope out of his shirt,
opened the envelope and tapped a white powder along
his left thumb. He put his nose to his thumb and sniffed,
drawing cocaine into his sinuses.

That felt a little bit better. He rolled his head around.
Just about ready to face the day. Squinting in preparation for the intense sun, he opened the garage door.

Goddamn Italian sun. Taylor, the garage door shut
behind him, stood on a cracked sidewalk and tried to
get his bearings. The Café Greco was to the left, he
remembered and started walking.

He didn't pay attention to the beat-up VW.

Kinsdale had been cruising the area around the
Café Greco for ninety minutes. Pozzuoli was a fishing
village ten miles out of Naples, a wayside of houses and
bars clumped on the edge of volcanic fields. Other
villages in the area had become thermal spas or excavations for sightseers. Pozzuoli had nothing of interest but a pseudo-café called the Greco. And, now,
Taylor.

Kinsdale drove slowly. Taylor, no doubt about it,
and looking vaguely at loose ends. At long last, the
target was in sight. Still, he noticed Taylor's hair
seemed to be short; the redheaded man he remembered
had long hair.

The VW passed Taylor. In his rearview mirror,
Kinsdale saw that Taylor's hair had been tied into a
bob at the back of his neck.

Kinsdale drove one more block before he stopped,
laid his .45 on his lap, then u-turned and, at a steady
four m.p.h., followed Taylor.

* * *

"An analysis from Rome," the technician entered Lupo's office.

Lupo glanced at Morrisey and accepted the new teletype.

"Ah," Lupo scanned the report, "they found what I wanted and more. At the Simpson site, I asked for photographs of all the tire tracks. Tracks were indeed found that matched tracks outside the Kinsdale house. Pirelli light-truck tires with an individual pattern of cut and worn tread marks. It seems, a physical analysis of the Simpson tracks also yielded traces of lava and sulfur dust."

"Meaning?"

"Naples. The terrorists' home is here," Lupo crossed to the map of the Bay of Naples on his wall. He checked the teletype again. "More exactly, here."

He pointed to an area on the coast north of Naples marked by the name "Campi Flegrei."

"The Phlegrean Fields," Lupo said. "The Mouth of Hell, we call it. A volcanic wasteland. The towns, Cumae, Misenum, Baia, Pozzuoli, Marechiaro, Bacoli, Bagnoli. Dozens of smaller places. Even with the Carabiniere, we wouldn't be able to cover them all."

"And I sent the task force to Rome," Morrisey cursed himself. "But I have more agents coming here this morning from Israel. Take them. Cover that area. Nothing happened last night, apparently. Maybe Kamal's decided to lie low for awhile and this is our chance. . . ."

The phone rang. Lupo answered it and offered the phone to Morrisey.

"It's for you. The embassy."

Morrisey wrote a note while he listened. Lupo read it while the telephone conversation progressed.

"Anon. call, 1123 hours—In retribution for last night's trap, Liberation forces will conduct mass slaughter tomorrow unless all conditions met."

Taylor had glanced back twice at the VW. He started walking faster. Kinsdale put a touch more weight on the accelerator.

The Café Greco was two more blocks down the street. No van was parked there. Hardly a soul was in sight anywhere. Every window he walked by, Taylor watched the looming reflection of the VW.

No Kamal, no Pidgeon. Where were they? Taylor looked down a street to the beach, where only grizzled fishermen attended torn nets. Despite the heat, Taylor was starting to feel very cold and scared. Taylor began running.

Kinsdale watched his target dart from the street into a cemetery. Marble angels, tombstones adorned with portraits set in glass, cherubim and seraphim hid the gangling running figure. There was no road, just a footpath. Kinsdale cut the wheel and ran the VW up the path.

A wall enclosed the rear of the cemetery. Taylor bounded over it with one leap and kept running into a haze-covered field.

Near the wall was the mound of a communal burial-ground during World War II. Scavenger dogs had attacked one end of the mound and unearthed white, brittle bones. Kinsdale shifted from second gear to third, racing the engine as he aimed for the mound. He hit the hump of earth at fifty m.p.h. The old Volkswagen rose into the air, soared over the four-foot wall and landed in a cloud of sulfurous dust.

Kinsdale shifted into first, drove out of the cloud and

aimed for Taylor, who was still running fifty feet ahead through wisps of sulfurous fumes.

Puffs of dust rose from Taylor's footsteps. Warm, acrid fog drifted like incense over the field. Kinsdale gunned the engine. There was no traction; the dust was like fine talcum. Taylor slipped, and looked back frantically. Kinsdale watched the gap between Taylor's feet and the VW's front bumper diminish to thirty feet, to fifteen.

Taylor leapt to the side. Kinsdale drove by, swung the wheel and the VW spun 180 degrees.

Taylor was on one knee, holding a Beretta. As Kinsdale closed on his target a second time, Taylor fired. The windshield of the VW crystalized as Kinsdale ducked. He opened his door and swung it, catching Taylor's arms and knocking the Beretta away.

The VW plowed by while Taylor scrambled for his gun. Kinsdale spun the car again. Taylor had the gun and was starting to aim. Kinsdale pulled his hood release. The hood popped up like a shield. He jerked the wheel left, sending the whole car into a sideways slide. Something hit the rear panel with a thud, and the only thing Kinsdale had seen on the field was Taylor.

Kinsdale stopped the VW and got out.

Taylor was lying on his back, his left pants leg split from his waist to his shoe. Kinsdale saw the Beretta fifty feet away. He reached down and pulled Taylor up by his hair.

"Taylor. Alexander Taylor?"

"I want a lawyer," Taylor gasped. "I don't say anything until I have a lawyer."

"Don't you know who I am?"

Taylor spat. Mucous covered Kinsdale's sunglasses and he took them off. Uncertainty filled Taylor's face, until he became sure and then he smiled.

"Yeah, yeah, I know you. The family man. You're not even a cop, you can't do anything to me."

Kinsdale yanked Taylor to his feet. Before the young man could smile again, Kinsdale drove five straightened fingers into Taylor's stomach. Taylor bent over and Kinsdale lifted a knee.

Taylor staggered back, his aquiline nose broken flush across his cheek. Blood spewed out down his chest.

"You're crazy."

"That's right."

Walking forward, he jabbed Taylor's mouth, crushing the lower incisors.

"Where are the others, Taylor?"

"I'm not going to tell you, you stupid . . ."

Still walking, almost strolling, Kinsdale leaned. The heel of his right shoe cut across Taylor's forehead, leaving the eyebrow hanging from a strip of skin.

"I don't know!" Taylor shouted.

"You can do better."

Moving forward, another kick. Taylor landed on his ass. He felt his ribs and his face.

"Please! I don't know. Who, who do you mean?"

"Where's Kamal?"

"I don't . . ." His face fell as he watched Kinsdale's arm draw back. "Wait, O.K., I'll tell, please, please. It was all their idea, everything, believe me. Just . . . help me up."

In control, Kinsdale told himself. The information was what he wanted. All available information was necessary to program the right plan. Helping Taylor up, too late he saw the switchblade snap out.

Taylor swung at Kinsdale's heart. Kinsdale blocked

the thrust, saw the long blade emerge four pink inches out the back of his hand. He staggered as Taylor ran for the car.

The blade was stuck. Deliberately, Kinsdale drew the knife out and threw it aside. The next moment, he was sprawled over the ground, which felt hollow, hot and inviting.

"You ignorant jerk," Taylor stood over him with a jack he'd taken from the VW's open hood. "How stupid can you be?"

Kinsdale rolled away as the jack came down, gouging the crusty lava. He rose to all fours, backing from Taylor.

"Don't you think we had fun in your house?" Taylor licked his bloody lip. "Just too bad you weren't there."

He swung. Kinsdale dove away, moving towards the car.

"Ignorant Fascist," Taylor swung again. Kinsdale dove for the hood of the VW. The jack came down like a club, but Kinsdale had rolled to the other side of the car. In his hand was a car chain.

"Pig!" Taylor thrust the jack at Kinsdale's eyes. Kinsdale sidestepped and, as Taylor stumbled, wrapped the chain around Taylor's neck. The jack dropped.

He held Taylor up by the chain and tightened it. Taylor gagged and reached back. Kinsdale wrapped a second loop around Taylor's neck. Taylor sagged and Kinsdale lifted him again until Taylor was on his tiptoes. Kinsdale's hands widened. Links twisted and dug into the reddened flesh of Taylor's neck. Blood pulsed out of Kinsdale's cut hand. Taylor's head contorted backward, his skin darkening. His legs shook. Kinsdale pulled the chain two links tighter. Taylor's whole body arched like a bow. Kinsdale saw his black face, Taylor's tongue protruding to his chin. With the last strength of his arms, Kinsdale pulled the chain one link tighter and Taylor's neck snapped loudly. Open bowels dripped urine and soil down the dead man's legs, and Kinsdale released the chain.

Where? he wondered, staring down at the pile that was Alexander Taylor.

"Where!" he kicked the dead man's ribs.

No answer.

Kinsdale shrugged, put his sunglasses back on and got into the car.

It takes two minutes to strangle a man to death, part of Kinsdale's brain remarked. Taylor only seemed to take seconds. Erroneous data, that part of Kinsdale's mind decided. Continue war game.

"More data came in while you were out," Morrisey told Lupo. "Rome says there are also traces of sea-water in that tire track."

Lupo went at once to his map.

"That eliminates the inland towns, then," the inspector said and pulled red pins from the center of the Phlegrean Fields. To Morrisey's surprise, Lupo also pulled pins from Cumae, Misenum, Bacoli, and Baia. "Too far a drive into Naples. Concentration is what we need . . . from Pozzuoli south."

"My new men are near Pozzuoli now. I can get them on their car radio."

"Good. This way we can examine every garage and courtyard."

Kinsdale backtracked from the Café Greco to where he'd first seen Taylor. There was a closed garage where Taylor had stood blinking into the sun in the last minutes of his life.

The garage door was unlocked. No vehicles were inside. Kinsdale waited for a solid ten minutes in the interior gloom, the .45 in his good hand, waiting for a sound. At last, he looked around. On the floor he found drops of blood and green paint, one unspent rifle round, and pieces of putty. In a corner, spray paint equipment, overalls daubed with paint and a stained bandage. This was the place.

Stairs led to a second floor. He climbed them, his gun held before him. Blocked by a door, he kicked it open and rushed in.

A loft. Living quarters. Cans of food, dirty aluminum utensils, magazines in a variety of languages, a table covered by an oil cloth and stray dominoes, a stuffed garbage can, seven mattresses on the floor. He counted the indentations. Eight people in all. Minus Taylor, back to seven. On the wall, maps of Italy, Rome and Naples. A mirror. Lying in one of the chairs . . . he squinted . . . a floppy ragdoll.

Shaggydo.

He picked up the doll and, holding it tight, sank into the chair. Tears started running down his cheeks. He rocked back and forth, crying.

If he had to wait a day or a year, he would. In the garage, holding the doll and the gun, waiting. And when they returned, he'd kill them all.

Late afternoon. The rattle of shopping carts mixed with childrens' voices. Country Squires, Pacer Hatchbacks, Club Wagons, Darts, Dusters dropped tail doors that bounced beneath Keds and paperbags of Cheerios, Pop Tarts, Tang, Pepsi, "New York Cut" sirloins, Cheer, Pream, Blue-Bonnet, Budweiser, Jack Daniels and Valium. Charcoal briquettes in a separate bag. A touch of Lip Gloss. Distribute the Trident. Seat belts. Ignition. The wives were going home.

Coming the other way, into the base commissary, was a van freshly painted Army green.

X

It was night and John Kinsdale realized they weren't coming back. He was waiting for no one.

His lethargy shaken off, he prowled the garage. He shook the magazines for notes, ripped open mattresses, opened the table drawers. Nothing. His eyes lighted on the overflowing garbage can.

He picked up the heavy can, lifted it over his head and threw it against the wall. Orange skins, bottles, tin cans, plastic bags and refuse covered the floor. On his knees, Kinsdale pored over the trash like a rag picker. Cigaret butts, picture postcards, fish bones. He extracted a damp napkin marked by ink. Carefully, he unfolded the napkin and spread it out. Written in a childish scrawl were the numbers, 567-884.

As Kinsdale straightened up, an arm locked around his neck. Like a sack, he was dragged up and rammed face-first into a wall. The arm cut off his air. The muzzle of a gun dug into his spine.

"He's got a gun, Abe!" the man holding him said.

"Right!"

Kinsdale felt his .45 being taken from his belt.

"Italiano?" the first man demanded in Kinsdale's ear.

"No . . ." Kinsdale struggled for breath. "Am . . . American."

"What the hell are you doing here, Mister?"

"Your arm . . ."

The second man was rifling Kinsdale's pockets.

"Oh, shit! Evan, let him go."

Released, Kinsdale sank along the wall. In the second man's hand was the plastic "Special Investigator's Identification" from the Ministry of the Interior. Abe, sharply dressed and lately tanned by the North African sun, looked at the card in disgust.

"Another one of ours. Goddamn, this job's a fuck-up."

This time, Evan's arm helped Kinsdale to his feet.

'Sorry, bud. What are you, Department of Defense?"

Dully, Kinsdale nodded. Abe handed the card back.

"What hapened to your hand?" he looked at the handkerchief around Kinsdale's hand.

"Arthritis." Kinsdale took his .45 back, too.

"Wonderful, a wise guy. That's Defense for you, a regular *Amateur Hour*. Mind telling us what's going on here? We've been in and out of more garages today than a dipstick thief."

CIA, Kinsdale figured, and they had to know pretty much to be hitting garages in Pozzuoli.

"Kamal's cleared out. Van's gone, no sign where to."

The operative called Evan kicked the trash on the floor.

"Might as well head back to the consulate and report in. You'll," he glanced at Kinsdale, "want to do the same thing, probably."

Outside, they all got into a blue Chevy, Abe behind the wheel. Kinsdale made no mention of the battered VW at the corner.

"The main thing," Abe said when they were underway back to Naples, "is where this 'mass slaughter' is supposed to take place tomorrow. The only place they'll find so many Americans together is on one of our warships parked in the bay. I'd like to see Kamal and his monkeys try to take on a destroyer. Evan, why don't you call in about the garage and our friend here?"

As Evan reached for the radio mike, Kinsdale stopped him.

"They have a shortwave receiver," Kinsdale said. "They're monitoring our calls."

"How do you know?"

"Found the manufacturer's guarantee in the waste can," Kinsdale lied.

Evan thought it over.

"Don't mind if we use it in our report, do you?"

"My pleasure."

"Thanks. Really sorry about the jostling, but the AIC has been barking at our asses ever since we landed."

"And there was a real good Marlon Brando movie on Beirut television tonight, too," Abe added. "Can't remember the title. Motorcycles and stuff. Good action."

"I thought you were a Doris Day fan," Evan said.

"You've got a dirty mind."

"Yeah, well, Alice doesn't think it's dirty enough. I just go home and crap out these days." Evan laughed. "We could be taking it easy Stateside, just bugging politicians."

The Chevy's headlights plunged ahead on the coast road to Naples. Kinsdale's bandaged hand squeezed the napkin with the numbers.

A telephone and a computer terminal were what he needed. Program Three was out and so was Lupo's data bank. The only linkup he could think of was at the consulate.

Night watchman Mario Lippi walked down a dimly lit row of peanut butters, jellies and jams toward the front of the commissary. The entire supermarket might have been lifted directly from the United States.

At the entrance were signs reading: *Authorized Personnel Only, Please Show Your Military Or Foreign Service I.D. At The Check-Out Counter, This Is Your Commissary—Help Keep It Clean,* and *Bargain! Just Arrived, Danley's American-Style English Muffins, 6 For 40¢.*

In his mind, Lippi made a shopping list of items to take home, because one of the advantages of working here was the shopping privileges. Even cheaper than the prices in the Vatican's commissary, he'd heard.

He hit the time clock and light switches. Around the vast store, blocks of lights flicked on and off. *Va Bene.* The next round would take him by the walk-in refrigerator and the service area, and then he could go back to his newspaper.

Lippi entered the swinging service door and flicked a switch. No light. He frowned; he didn't feel like climbing a ladder to change the bulb. He took the flashlight off his belt and swung it around.

The refrigerator door was shut and its thermostat was at the right temperature. No power breakdown. Sacks of flour and sugar were stacked neatly. Never any rats, you had to give that to the Americans. The electric fork-lift truck was plugged into the wall.

The flashlight's beam picked out the door to the

truck bay, where deliveries were unloaded during the day. The metal door was not only open, it was buckled and hanging from its hinges.

A sugar sack tumbled to the floor.

"Chi?" Lippi asked.

Someone punched him in the stomach. The night watchman stepped back to the wall. Such a punch. He could barely draw his breath. He turned his flashlight on his stomach. The long handle of a knife stuck out below his ribs. Like a stage prop, a play knife, he thought. A joke.

Mario Lippi sank to his knees and then onto his side. Another knife, as real as the first one, plunged into his back, but he was already dead.

Rubber-soled shoes jumped over him. Hooded figures rushed through the service door into the main commissary area. Working the breeches of their automatic rifles, they fanned out and each padded up an aisle.

At the front of the supermarket, they gathered under a sign reading: *Remember. You Are Guests In This Country—Do Not Abuse Your Privileges.*

When they arrived at the consulate, Abe and Evan left Kinsdale in the front hall. He started for the consul's office, but as soon as they were out of sight he slipped into a stairwell and down to the basement communications center.

"This is off limits, Sir," said the young man who opened the Data Room's fireproof door. "The information desk is on the first floor."

"Edmondson," Kinsdale flashed his stolen pass. "I'm coordinating for the task force and the Italians."

"I could do that," the programmer opened the door reluctantly.

"When you had the special clearance," Kinsdale walked in, "which would take a day. Let's see what you've got here."

He crossed to a computer/display/printout system that took up a third of the small room.

"You know how to use these?" the programmer asked.

"IBM 1130s with a 2250 display. Yeah, I think I can handle it."

The kid picked up his sports jacket and threw it over his shoulder with a mutter. It occurred to Kinsdale the last thing he needed was a petulant programmer asking questions upstairs about the stranger who moved him out of the Data Room.

"Look, you want to be a help? We don't have a man we can trust at the airport. It's a little dangerous," Kinsdale added in an offhand way.

"Yeah?" the kid's eyes lit up.

"If you see a group of men carrying leather satchels marked *Aero Tours* call here immediately and ask for Agatha. Don't try to apprehend them yourself. And don't discuss this with anyone on your way out of here."

"You can depend on me," the kid almost saluted and ran out.

Kinsdale waited a second and locked the door.

A piece of the action was all the kid wanted. Gibberish made it all the easier to swallow. And now Kinsdale was at home with the last allies he could count on. The machines he knew best. Because the enemy was no army moving through an airport, but phantoms hiding among magnetic tapes.

From the racks of tapes, he chose one labeled "NAPLES—MUNI." and threaded it into the 1130's drive capstan. The tape self-threaded through the head assembly.

"IDENTIFY TELE. 567-884," he punched out on the console.

Tape streamed through the eye of the head assembly. Kinsdale watched it stop when it reached the Naples telephone directory and then chugged through the million or more imprinted numbers and names in seconds.

"CROSS REF. NATO PERS." appeared on the console display.

The NATO personnel file? he wondered. Was Kamal really ready to take on a military installation?

He put the new tape on and punched out the same command. His answer came before he sat back.

"NATO BASE COMMISSARY, NAPLES, TELE. 567-884, 885, 886."

Kamal was counting the commissary's day shift on the manager's pay sheet when the office phone rang. Pidgeon ran in, whitefaced.

"Alex, you think?"

"He doesn't know where we are," Kamal frowned.

The phone rang for the fourth time. Kamal tapped his fingers on the manager's desk.

"Maybe it's the police calling?" she asked.

"More likely the manager trying to reach the watchman. Or the watchman's wife. Or a wrong number. It doesn't matter," he said angrily, "because we're not answering and we're not going anyplace."

On the tenth ring, Kinsdale hung up.

The commissary. Not one family this time, a hundred families.

He needed a game map. The layouts of all base buildings were stored in the 1130s at Program Three. He pushed DISPLAY and began typing.

"SOUTHERN FORCES—ITALY. INSERT KEY CODES," the display answered.

Kinsdale punched out the code for Program Three and using the console phone, dialed the number of his terminal console at Program Three.

"Program Three," Mike answered.

Kinsdale laid the receiver aside and punched out MANUAL BYPASS.

"Program Three," Mike tried again, and hung up. It didn't matter, as long as Kinsdale's phone at the consulate was off the hook the link was made.

"LOCATE AND DISPLAY . . ." Kinsdale began.

Half a cigaret later, the 2250 display unit was reproducing a white-on-black architect's layout of the USSF Bay of Naples commissary.

Public area with ten aisles, frozen food chillers, checkout counters. Service area of meat refrigerator, storing, unloading. Manager's office. Electrical wiring, heating and air conditioning attachments to outside generator and AC shed. Doors, windows, unloading bays.

The 2250 was an "interactive" console with its own memory disk of geometric shapes. Kinsdale punched in triangular prisms for the foodshelves, raised the narrow prisms to six feet; replaced the flat drawing of chillers with hexahedrons, counters with rhomboids, checking and counter-checking with architectural specifications, so that in minutes he had an exact three-dimensional model of the commissary.

"ROTATE 360 DEGREES," he punched.

As if the display were an eye turning in the middle of the commissary, even to preprogrammed effects of optical distortion, aisles and counters slowly swung across the display. There were seven killers, he remembered. Judiciously, as if the turning eye were Kamal's, he placed the seven phantoms where they would be needed most.

"CLEAR. LOCATE AC DATA. . . ."

The next job was the seemingly prosaic one of defining the dimensions of the commissary's air conditioning ducts.

It was five in the morning when Kinsdale had the game plan he wanted. He left the Data Room and walked up to the first floor stairwell.

Voices could be heard from the hall. The entire consulate was on twenty-four hour alert because of the latest ultimatum. He listened to the agent called Evan talking to someone else he recognized.

"The guy said he was from Defense. No one told us about a stolen ID."

"Well, now you know and you better find him. Christ, Rome, Pozzuoli, and here!" George Edmonds fumed. "It's lucky I did come down here."

"But how does he know where to go if he's not . . ." Evan's voice trailed away.

Kinsdale opened the door a crack. Edmonds and Evan turned a corner at the end of the hall. Kinsdale slipped into the corridor and out an exit marked, "To Garage."

A fleet of big American sedans was parked in the gloom of the consulate garage. Kinsdale picked out a black Ford with Rome plates. The keys were in the Ford's ignition and when he reached under the seat, he found Edmond's sawed-off shotgun. Kinsdale slid in.

On the second floor of the consulate, Edmonds was waiting by a window while his call to Rome was being put through. He looked at the headlights of a car coming out of the garage. As it swung into the street, he saw the car's license number.

"That bastard!" Edmonds shouted futilely. "That crazy bastard!"

The night watchman's body lay under a mound of flour sacks. The door to the truck bay was bolted shut and Kamal stationed a man at the service door.

Hurrying now—the commissary employees would be arriving soon—Kamal oversaw the preparations at the front of the checkout counters. Plastic C-4 explosive had been attached at intervals along the walls. Detonated, the high-order explosive would produce shock waves with a velocity of 25,000 feet per second. No one would be alive to see the roof overhead erupt like the cap of a volcano.

First, Kamal knew, would come the "shattering effect" on everything within a fifty-yard radius of the building. Cement, stainless steel, tin cans and flesh, disintegrated, would rise in a thousand-foot pillar of smoke. Throughout the whole Bay of Naples, gulls would rise squawking into the sky. Then, the terrible debris would start falling into the narrow alleys of the city, across the docks, into the blue water.

One of his men tried to attach the joined wires of the plastic to the detonator.

"Here," Kamal brushed him aside, "let me. This has to be done exactly right."

Lupo's police sedan rolled into the checkpoint of Program Three, where the guards, alerted to his arrival, waved him through. Janice met the chief inspector at the door, eased his passage by the marines on guard and led him to the elevators.

"Mr. McAllister called me," Lupo said as they stepped into the elevator. "Can you tell me why?"

"I'd rather he did," she avoided an answer. "Can you tell me why you came?"

"Gladly," Lupo said, but more bitterly than with pleasure. "I've come to realize I had no choice. Your friend Kinsdale has consistently been one, sometimes ten, steps ahead of us. Plainly, his resources are greater than ours. Isn't it time the proper authorities used those resources?"

She liked the Italian, but Janice could tell he was being as evasive as she was.

"Is that all?" she asked.

"No," he admitted. "I've also came to the conclusion that when I find your friend, I will also find the people he is after."

The elevator doors parted and they entered the War Room. Lupo took a deep breath. He had shown the police computer room to Kinsdale? The Naples Criminal Data Bank could fit into a shelf of Program Three and never be found again. Luminescent maps alive with menacing blips surrounded the huge interior. Directly across, on a screen only twenty feet across, was a color projection of himself, a portrait beside his name and a confidential biography he would have sworn to his mother could never be read by anyone but a chief of police.

Down in the concave center of the War Room was a man at a console.

"That's him," Mike McAllister shouted. "Bring him on down."

"How?" Lupo asked angrily when he reached Mike.

"That?" Mike followed Lupo's gaze to the portrait on the screen. "Oh, this terminal is connected to Program Three's 1130s. The 1130 computers are interrogating the 1047 computers at the Interpol Collective in Brussels."

"How can it do that? That's classified police material."

"Doctor Lupo," Mike said kindly, "Program Three is designed to get classified material. Please, have a seat. I only did that to make sure the right man was going to come through the door."

Slightly mollified, Lupo sat at the console next to Mike's.

"But it points up why I called you," Mike said. "This," he gestured to the War Room, "Program Three, it's all pretty much John Kinsdale's baby. He is one of the most talented computer programmers around, he's also one of the most imaginative war gamers alive. A rare combination."

"A dangerous one."

Mike nodded.

"True. I don't know why I underestimated him. We . . . we began gathering information from Program Three together when he started seeking facts about the killers of Ann and his kids. I stopped helping him a couple of days ago shortly before he had that incident with you. Since then, I've been rather a camper here, sitting on Program Three so that John wouldn't be able to make a computer link, so that he wouldn't be able to get any more data from Program Three and he'd give up on all this."

"Yes?"

"Then, tonight, I answered the phone on John's console, the one you're sitting at. No one answered and I hung up. About an hour ago, I started thinking about that call and getting worried. I went down into the computer galley myself and checked the energy meters. Then I came right back and called you."

"What do you mean?"

"John was the phone caller and he was calling from a terminal. When I picked up the phone, he managed to bypass his console and make a direct hookup. All the time I was sitting up here waiting, he was pulling information out of the guts of Program Three. I don't know what the information was. I do know from the meters, he took a lot."

The door to the War Room burst open and General Fuller strode in, buttoning his tunic.

"This is a Top Secret area. What's this I hear about visitors without clearance?"

Mike, usually cowed by the general's bluster, regarded Fuller with steady coolness.

"General Fuller, this is Chief Inspector Lupo."

Fuller shook hands brusquely and turned back to Mike.

"You asked him here? Have you heard of a chain of command?"

"This is police business," Lupo said.

"*Local* police business," Fuller said.

"General," Janice spoke up. "This concerns John Kinsdale."

"Oh, that matter of placing him under protective custody?"

"General Fuller," Mike said firmly, "John and I have been using Program Three to find the people who killed his family."

"A very elaborate vendetta, I'm afraid," murmured Lupo.

"Oh . . ." the wind went out of Fuller. "And?"

"We think John may have found them," Mike replied. "We hope he will try to reach Program Three when he does. So we're waiting for the call."

"Or for the casualties," Lupo looked at the tote-boards.

XI

A warm, Italian morning sun bathed the concrete expanse of the base. At the commissary, newly-arrived employees chattered as they doffed jackets. A girl rang her register. When the drawer popped open, she broke a roll of coins. In the parking lot, the first wave of American station wagons were parking, a wave larger than usual because today was Saturday and families wanted to get their shopping done to clear the rest of their time for the beach.

"*Dove Mario?*" the commissary manager wandered among the employees.

No one had seen the night watchman. Probably the old man had an upset stomach and went home early, the manager had decided. He headed for his office.

A curly-haired butcher ran in the door and kissed one of the cashiers on the hand. She whispered in his ear.

"*Va Bene,*" he started for the service area in the rear of the commissary.

In his office, the manager checked his watch: 7:59. He took a tape cassette from his desk and slipped it into a player. His finger leaned on Play. Throughout the supermarket, the sprightly, slightly inane melody of prerecorded Muzak flowed from a public address system.

The commissary was fast filling up with customers. Toddlers were put in shopping cart seats. Their bigger brothers and sisters ran for the family packs of soda and candy. At the cold cuts section, carts loaded down with an assortment of local pastrami and imported liverwurst.

"Fresh in today," a recorded announcement broke into the Muzak, "Cobber Farms Prime American Turkey Breasts. This is a commissary special at the frozen meats chest."

Some of the customers were already going through the checkout counters. One cashier turned over a cellophane-wrapped leg of lamb searching for a price mark.

"A moment."

Carrying the meat, she started looking for the curly-headed butcher.

The manager was doing some needless tidying along the frozen juice chest when he noticed in the back of the chest a wire running into something like putty stuck onto the wall. Some new electrical work he hadn't even been told about. He had half a mind to rip the wire right off the wall.

As the cashier pushed up the service door, she heard a clatter of meat hooks hitting the floor.

"*Ugo!*" she laughed. "*Ugo! Che fa guel scemo?*"

Ugo came out of the meat locker. His shirt from his collar to his belt was torn open, as was his chest and stomach. His clothes looked as if they'd been dyed deep scarlet and he held his hands over the glistening pulp of bared intestines. His eyes wide, his mouth gaping, Ugo dropped at her feet.

As the figures in black hoods rushed out of the locker, she screamed.

At the front of the commissary, a lone, hooded man closed the doors. He turned and sprayed the ceiling with automatic rifle fire. Rifle fire answered from the rear, setting off a general panic of screaming. Shopping carts overturned. Grape juice bottles piled high on a shelf exploded with a gush of purple glass.

Hooded by gray woolen socks with holes for eyes, dressed in uniform gray sweaters, padding in sneakers, Kamal's men spread out, each waving his G-3. Women dragging their children from the hooded figure at one end of the aisle ran into another hooded man at the other.

And the Muzak droned on.

"With summer coming on," an unconcerned announcement reminded, "who can resist fresh Florida orange juice? Stock up today while the supply lasts. Take advantage of our special spring discount on all frozen juices."

Screaming had turned to whimpering and stunned silence. In every aisle, women, children and cashiers lay prostrate as the hooded men stepped over them. At the front of the commissary, one figure jumped onto a checkout counter.

"Nobody must move until I say," Kamal shouted. "You will die if you move."

Nobody, he could see, was going to stir. In Aisle Three, a young mother who hadn't been able to disentangle a baby from a shopping cart seat knelt by the cart and hugged her baby defiantly, but as still as a rock. From different sections of the supermarket rose the crying of children.

"Who is in charge?" Kamal demanded.

There was no immediate response. Kamal lowered his rifle towards the baby in the cart.

"I said, who . . ."

"I am," the commissary manager answered from the floor of Aisle Two.

"Come here!"

The manager got to his feet. As he moved toward Kamal, he whispered encouragement to his customers. Don't worry . . . it will be all right . . . some mistake. Blanched by his own fear, he delivered himself to the counter where Kamal stood.

Kamal produced a folded piece of paper and gave it to the manager.

"You will go to the guards. Explain the situation here and say you must give the paper to the base commander. Tell them, also, if they approach the commissary we will kill everyone here. We have killed and *will* kill. Tell them," Kamal's eyes glowed with fervor, "we are not afraid to die."

If the computer hadn't told him it was possible, Kinsdale would have given up. The duct between the air conditioning shed and the back of the commissary was fifteen feet long. His shoulders squeezed together, he inched his way forward. Blindly, he unscrewed the baffles he met, obstacles he had studied on the consulate terminal's display. Then, inched ahead, listening to the duct's tinny echo of automatic arms fire. Minutes later, he heard the discordant wailing of sirens.

The thinnest hint of light lay ahead. Kinsdale forced himself to worm his way as slowly as before, with infinite care, not letting the .45 and the sawed-off shot-gun in his belt touch the duct, not allowing the slightest sound to announce his arrival.

When Lupo, Mike and Janice crossed the base from the War Room, a cordon had already been set up around the entire commissary. Squads of marines massed behind a ring of armored personnel carriers. Overhead, missile-carrying Huey helicopters hovered 200 feet above the commissary roof. Along the far end of the parking lot, base officers, many of whom had families inside the commissary, were restrained by more marines. Carabiniere held back gathering Nea-politans on the exterior road.

"This is it," Morrisey jumped off a passing jeep to tell Lupo. "Kamal."

Lupo saw a limousine flying an American flag cruise up to Fuller and a group of other generals. Edmonds and the American consul got out of the car.

"He wants ten million dollars in cash, half the pris-ons in West Europe thrown open, and safe conduct to an Arab state."

"What will happen?"

"Well," Morrisey threw up his hands, "those mur-derers have over a hundred American hostages in there and Italian employees as well. We land on that roof or drive through the doors and Kamal threatens to blow the whole goddamn place up."

"He would do it," Lupo looked at the futile ranks of soldiers.

"Have you found John Kinsdale?" Janice asked.

"Who cares about that nut?" Morrisey blew up. "Right now we're arranging the money and the plane. As for the prisoners he wants released, I don't know

what the hell we're going to do. And the toughest
thing now is to keep the husbands of those hostages
from trying to rush in there."

A fleet of ambulances rolled into the lot. News service vans established themselves on the exterior road,
film crews setting themselves up on the roofs of the
vans. At least a hundred yards separated the armed
cordon from the commissary.

"You are a war gamer," Lupo said to Mike. "What
would you do?"

"Surrender."

"But that won't be good enough," Janice said. "No
matter what we give them, they'll need all the prisoners
released so they'll have sufficient prestige to be wel-
comed in the Mideast. That factor we don't control and
the Europeans will never set free a thousand convicted
killers. We'll negotiate with Kamal as long as we can,
but . . . in the end, he'll kill everyone."

Lupo nodded. The young woman was right. Then he
noticed the man called Edmonds pointing towards a
black Ford parked beside the air conditioning shed at
the commissary.

"Perhaps," the police inspector said, "there's one
more factor. . . ."

XII

The terrorist on guard in the service area was called through the service doors.

Kinsdale pushed out the ventilation grille and squirmed from the duct, dropping onto a mound of sugar sacks. Three of the sacks rolled aside, revealing the body of a fat old man with a watchman's ring of keys. Beside the service door were two more bodies, one of a young man and the other of a cashier. Kinsdale moved quickly into the cab of the fork-lift truck, pulling his head down as the guard came back.

The hooded man slipped a padlock on the service doors. As soon as he turned, though, he spotted the moved sacks.

"Who's there?"

Kinsdale threw the truck's lever to Full-Forward. Rifle fire tore into the sacks behind the truck, spewing cascades of sugar. Kinsdale raised the lift on the moving truck. The terrorist held his ground. Shells ricocheted from the truck's steel snout.

The lift's sharp edge caught the terrorist at the neck. Carrying him, the truck rammed into the service doors. Blood from a crushed larynx spread from a mouth, giving the woolen mask a red beard. The padlock burst and the truck bulled into the commissary's main area. Kinsdale rolled out of the cab while, on its own, the truck carried its corpse into a metal soda cooler. The body dropped to the floor. The head stayed pinned to the lift.

Another terrorist appeared around the cooler and stopped in horror. From the other side of the truck, Kinsdale stuck his shotgun in the second man's belt and fired. Buckle, sweater wool, viscera, bone and blood erupted from a foot-wide exit wound over a display of pet food.

"What's happening in there?" Lupo demanded.

"I don't know." General Fuller took the radio mike from a personnel carrier. "All troops will hold their positions, but get ready for assault. Helicopter pilots will approach to one hundred feet. Do not land, repeat, do not hit the roof until the order is given."

"It sounds like a war in there," Morrisey said.

In fact, the firing had stopped. Muzak wafted through the commissary, punctuated only by the sobbing of small children.

Kinsdale moved up Aisle Four—cleaning products. From the floor, huddled women watched him with a mixture of terror and hope. At the far end of the aisle, by the checkout counters, was a plunger-type detonator he wanted to keep an eye on.

But that was their last resort. Now they'd stalk him, as he was stalking them. Two down and five to go. He held the shotgun in his right hand and the .45 in his bandaged left hand.

"Mommy," a boy cringed.

Boxes of detergent spun off the top of the shelf like shooting gallery ducks. More rifle fire, so close it was deafening, swept through, shattering bottles of bleach.

Crouched, Kinsdale looked up at a curved anti-shop-lifting mirror. In the next aisle, a terrorist was in the middle of switching clips in his rifle. Kinsdale stood abruptly and tapped the top of the aisle divider with his shotgun.

The terrorist stood in surprise eye-level with the shotgun's two barrels. Kinsdale fired. A bloody mask flew like a red flag into the air.

Kinsdale dropped the empty shotgun and transferred the .45 to his good hand. Three down. He started running down the aisle to the detonator.

Some serviceman's grandmother was huddled against a rack of mops. She screamed as Kinsdale ran towards her. Too late, he realized she was screaming not at him, but at something behind him. He spun.

A terrorist had climbed the divider between Aisles Four and Three. Standing, he fired his G-3.

Kinsdale was slammed back into the mops, his blood spattering the old woman. On his side, he fired. Hitting the terrorist in the middle of his chest, the .45 shell lifted him over the aisle and onto the next divider. His rifle skidded over linoleum.

A round had gone through the meat of Kinsdale's thigh. He pulled himself up and limped ahead of a red trail.

"Attention, please!" a voice announced. "Today only, a special sale on Schlitz beer. Get your case while they last. Thank you."

* * *

"Bring the choppers down," Fuller shouted into the mike. "A recoilless rifle at the front door, then gas grenades in the launchers."

"I heard automatic fire in there. What was the other sound?" Janice asked.

"A shotgun. My shotgun," Edmonds said. The consul looked at him with alarm. "I just wish I could have pulled the trigger," Edmonds added.

They'd have him pinpointed by now, Kinsdale knew. Aisle Four would be blocked at both ends and he and every hostage in the aisle would be chopped down. Limping, he remembered the computer's model of the commissary. For every hundred feet of permanent aisle divider there was ten feet of rollaway divider.

Under shelves of fruit cocktail, canned peaches and cherries, his eyes picked out casters. With a grunt, he heaved himself against the shelves. They rolled back, hit something and toppled. Two hundred pounds of cans swung down into the next aisle, followed by Kinsdale falling from his own momentum.

Trapped beneath the shelf, but raising his rifle was another terrorist. Kinsdale whipped the barrel of his gun across the mask and the rifle fell away. He held the .45 against the terrorist's ear and pulled off the mask. Long blonde hair came out of the hood and the face he was aiming at was a pretty girl's.

His finger slid off the trigger. The girl was smiling. So young, Kinsdale thought. Almost innocent. But the smile turned to a sneer.

"He's here, Kamal!" she shouted. "He's . . ."

Kinsdale's bandaged fist smashed into Pidgeon's

jaw. Her head lolled sideways, unconscious. He heard feet running to her call.

He moved down the aisle, dragging his bleeding leg over the body of the terrorist he'd shot with the .45. The leg kept betraying him. In front of the prostrate customers, he staggered into one shelf after another.

"They're on the roof," Fuller watched marines dropping from rope ladders onto the commissary. "Start moving in. Keep your men behind the vehicles!"

The cordon closed. The recoilless rifle, a cannon set on the chassis of a scout car, rolled to the commissary door ahead of assault troops in gas masks. From all sides of the building, personnel carriers advanced before more men.

Lupo heard yelling. At the far end of the lot, servicemen had broken through the marines. The line of Carabiniere had been breached as well by their countrymen swarming in from the exterior road.

"Shoot to kill," Fuller was saying into his mike, "kill anyone armed."

"General, John is in there," Janice yelled.

"I know," Fuller put his hand over the mike, "I know that."

Kinsdale tripped and fell again. The .45 spun down the aisle.

"Quick! Here!" a voice whispered. "There's one coming."

Next to a baby in a shopping cart was a young mother holding a G-3. From the man he'd shot on the divider, Kinsdale realized. He crawled towards her.

Someone vaulted a divider and landed in the aisle behind Kinsdale. The baby in the cart cried with fright.

Footsteps charged closer. Kinsdale stretched his hand out for the rifle. A bullet ripped through his shoulder, flattening him. Helpless, he twisted onto his back to see the man who was going to kill him.

In full-stride, the terrorist ran into a fusillade of heavy caliber rounds tearing into him on a diagonal from hip to shoulder. He sank against a cardboard display of an American family hoisting glasses of instant tea. The G-3 kept firing, cutting through the terrorist and the display until he fell back into chewed cardboard and he and the display collapsed together.

Kinsdale turned painfully onto his good leg. The woman by the shopping cart was still aiming the automatic rifle, her finger still clamped to the trigger while the G-3's breech clicked on an empty chamber. Tears of shock and self-horror covered her face. Kinsdale pulled the rifle out of her grip.

"I murdered him," she gasped.

"You picked a good time to do it," Kinsdale said softly.

Kamal Hamshari ran to the checkout end of Aisle Five, straining to catch the direction of Kinsdale's voice.

"Attention, Florida orange juice and grapefruit juice, our spring special, are marked . . ."

Kamal held his hands over his ears to blot out the idiotic recording.

". . . Ten cents for the coming holidays. That's ten . . ."

Kamal couldn't keep the words out of his head. He aimed at the closest loudspeaker and fired until the speaker hung from its wire, but still the voice echoed from half a dozen other speakers.

". . . Ten days left. Buy 'em now. Thank you."

His head jerked up. Feet were running over the roof. A trapdoor directly overhead dropped open. Kamal emptied the last of his clip through the opening and the door slapped shut.

Except for the strains of Muzak, the supermarket had become deathly quiet.

"Abdul!" Kamal shouted anxiously. "Amin? Yasir? . . . Pidgeon?"

No answer. He was alone, the last one. On the floor, the Americans stared at him.

"You'll do," he yanked a girl from the floor by her arm. He dropped the empty rifle and held a machine pistol against the back of her head. "You'll do just as I say. We'll walk slowly to the front door."

The girl winced and nodded.

Together, they moved to the end of the aisle, toward the checkout counters.

Because he could still win, Kamal told himself. With one glorious act, he could still prove he was someone to be listened to, still be famous as well dead as alive.

John Kinsdale had dragged himself to his .45, and then to the end of the aisle. His shoulder blade was broken, his left arm totally useless. In a prone position, he rested the big automatic on a bag of cat sand. In the .45's sights was the detonator.

Two figures, Kamal and the shield of a girl, entered Kinsdale's field of vision. Kinsdale swung the barrel's sights to Kamal, but the girl was struggling, giving Kinsdale no clear shot. If they continued to the door, he wouldn't get a shot at all.

Kamal stopped and leaned on the detonator plunger. The detonator shattered and kicked out of his hand. The girl yanked free. Kamal turned, facing Kinsdale's second shot.

Kinsdale fired again. Kamal pitched backward over the counter.

From every aisle, the hostages rose and ran to the front door of the commissary. Dragging their children, they streamed by Kinsdale and out the door, a flood of liberated pandemonium that mingled with the rush of startled soldiers.

Kinsdale pulled himself to his feet.

Under the counter, Kamal felt the blood pumping from his side. Feet ran by him. He retrieved his pistol and pulled the woolen mask from his head. From the counter, he joined the crush at the door, integrating with them, hiding among his former hostages.

Kamal! Kinsdale saw the darkly handsome face pressing through the crowd. Limping, one arm hanging, he followed.

The mass movement from the commissary met another one of American and Italian husbands and fathers. Personnel carriers were abandoned. Fuller's command carrier was isolated in a swirl of general confusion. Only Lupo seemed to be aware of the tattered and bloody figure staggering last out of the supermarket.

"Kamal!" Kinsdale yelled.

Kamal had fallen to his knees. A pink foam oozed from his mouth. His pistol was on the parking lot ground and he felt for it as if blind.

"Kamal!"

A human circle widened around the wounded terrorist. Others edged away from Kinsdale.

"John, don't," Janice screamed.

Lupo forced his way through the crowd.

A harsh bubbling sound came from Kamal's throat. He found his gun and concentrated on it, as if the motor responses of his hand were dead.

"Kamal!"

Staggering, his own clothes torn and caked with blood, no less grotesque than something semi-human, Kinsdale stood over the terrorist. Kamal looked up, his head tilted sleepily, his eyes unfocused.

Kinsdale knelt and put the .45 at Kamal's temple.

"No!" Lupo broke through the circle around the two bloody men. "No, Kinsdale."

A light of understanding touched Kamal's eyes. His fingers pawed the butt of his gun. Heavy foam gushed from his mouth with the effort to pick the gun up. The hammer of Kinsdale's .45 eased back.

"No, Kinsdale," Lupo said. "He's dead."

Kinsdale touched Kamal's shoulder. The terrorist rolled over, blank eyes staring into the sun. Dead, all but the brain, which died last and in which flickered one final electric impulse to pick up a gun and shoot.

Kinsdale dropped the .45 as arms lifted him to his feet. Lupo was pushing the crowd back. Janice's face appeared, and Mike's. They spoke but Kinsdale couldn't make out what they said through the babble of the lot. The sunglasses fell from his face and he blinked from the glare of the day. He was terribly wounded, he knew, but he felt no pain. Part of that could be explained by shock, but not all. General Fuller floated into view with a gladhand of congratulations.

"Thank you."

Those words pierced his mind. There was a young mother holding a baby. A Navy lieutenant was at her side. Kinsdale vaguely pictured her with a rifle.

Lupo and McAllister carried Kinsdale to an ambulance. Salt. Kinsdale licked his lips. He was crying as he looked back at the family. Now he remembered why.

Across the lot, the station wagons were pulling out. From the commissary doors, the crowd dispersed. Forensic teams and photographers busied themselves with notepads and pictures. Around Kamal was a white chalk line. But everyone else was going home.

The war game was over.

THE SWEENEY

Ian Kennedy Martin

Jack Regan is one of the Heavy Mob.
He's also a loner, intolerant of red tape and
insubordinate to his superiors.
And he just happens to be the best detective in
Scotland Yard's crack Flying Squad.

When Regan receives orders to co-operate with
Lieutenant Ewing, over from America to trace a cop
killer, Regan is pursuing his own case and ignores
them. But he soon discovers that Ewing is as tough as
he is – and a dangerous clash of personalities
develops. As the two cases begin to merge into a
sinister and violent network of IRA provos and
murderers, the two men close in for the kill . . .

Ian Kennedy Martin is the creator of Thames
Television's enormously popular TV series, starring
John Thaw.

MAN FRIDAY

Adrian Mitchell

In MAN FRIDAY Adrian Mitchell retells Defoe's famous classic ROBINSON CRUSOE through the eyes of Friday, Crusoe's 'savage' companion.

When Friday is washed ashore after a storm with others of his tribe, he alone survives a brutal attack by Crusoe. He is then taken as Crusoe's slave who attempts to civilize him. But as Friday strives to understand his captor's strange whims and emotions, it becomes apparent that Crusoe has no more right to be the master than Friday is the savage.

And slowly, inexorably, as the relationship develops, Friday learns to assert himself and the story ends, as it begins, in stark tragedy ...

MAN FRIDAY is now a powerful film directed by Jack Gold and starring Peter O'Toole and Richard Roundtree.

THE ULTRA SECRET

F. W. Winterbotham

'The greatest British Intelligence coup of the Second World War has never been told till now'
Daily Mail

For thirty-five years the expert team of cryptanalysts who worked at Bletchley Park have kept the secret of how, with the help of a Polish defector, British Intelligence obtained a precise copy of the highly secret and complex German coding machine known as Enigma, and then broke the coding system to intercept all top-grade German military signals. Group-Captain Winterbotham was the man in charge of security and communication of this information. Now he is free to tell the story of that amazing coup and what it uncovered.

'A story as bizarre as anything in spy fiction . . . the book adds a new dimension to the history of World War II'
New York Times

'Military historians, like the general reader, will be astonished by this book . . . Group-Captain Winterbotham cannot be too highly commended'
The Listener

'Superbly told'
Daily Express

MAHLER

Kurt Blaukopf

Mahler: the child prodigy who was composing at the age of four; the musician whose genius anticipated the great era of stereophonic recording; the conductor who revolutionised concert hall and opera house; the man whose symphonies inspired Thomas Mann's DEATH IN VENICE.

Kurt Blaukopf traces the story of Mahler's life and work against its background of the disintegrating Austro-Hungarian Empire, though his relationships with the three women he loved, his battle to win directorship of the Vienna Court Opera to the final breakdown and the crisis of his meeting with Freud a year before his death. An outstanding study of the man whose work is a landmark in twentieth-century music.